# LOOKING FOR MR. RIGHT

ROSE MARIE MEUWISSEN

*Looking for Mr. Right*
Digital/Print Edition
Copyright 2023 by Rose Marie Meuwissen
https://www.rosemariemeuwissen.com

Print ISBN: 978-1-954030-04-6
Published in the United States of America
Nordic Publishing
Edited by Leanore Elliot and
Rose Marie Meuwissen
Cover Design by Rose Marie Meuwissen

nordic
PUBLISHING

❀ Created with Vellum

# DEDICATION

*To my Mr. Right, Dennis Bartholow, who happened to be looking for his perfect match on the same online dating service I was on. Thankfully, he was looking for his last girlfriend.*

# BLURB

*Rocki*

Internet dating wasn't something Rocki Sandstrom ever thought she would try. When her best friend insisted, they set up online profiles to search for Mr. Right. Only because she was positive it wouldn't work. But when Rocki literally met Mr. Wrong who suggested there was nothing wrong with having a little fun while she kept looking for Mr. Right, she actually saw some truth in the idea. What could it hurt?

Will Rocki find her Mr. Right? Or will she only find Mr. Wrong?

*Dominick*

Dominick Taggart believed internet dating couldn't possibly help anyone find their person. He felt so strongly about it that he decided to write his Master's Thesis on it. The only way to get first-hand knowledge on the subject was to sign up for Life Match Dating. His theory was that women looked for Mr. Right but wanted Mr. Wrong. Why couldn't he be both?

Will Dominick be proved wrong and actually find his person?

# A MINNESOTA LAKES ROMANCE

*Looking for Mr. Right*

*by*

*Rose Marie Meuwissen*

# CHAPTER 1

"*I* deserve a man who wants only me!" Rocki Sandstrom faced the mirror to check out the reflection of the woman staring back at her. Hell, she looked damn good, still! After all, she was only a little over forty. Dang, but she felt old these days, even though she still looked hot. At least, she thought so. What was wrong with her that she couldn't find a man? Well, it definitely wasn't because she hadn't found any, because she had. Unfortunately for both her and them, she just didn't like any of them. Enough, that was. Actually, it wasn't that they weren't likeable, they simply didn't make her blood run hot. Not even warm. She wanted blood to rush through her entire body in a heated response to a man's touch.

"Rocki? You ready to go?" Allisa asked, as she walked in through the front door of Rocki's lavish two-story executive house in Prior Lake.

"Coming!" Rocki yelled down, above the railing overlooking the front foyer. "I'll be down in a minute."

"You look great. In fact, you look hot!" Allisa walked into the great room adjoining the kitchen and took a seat on a stool at the breakfast bar.

Rocki picked out a matching black leather purse with lots of gold bling to go with her outfit of black skin tight jeans tucked into three-inch heeled black leather boots, also boasting gold bling. Then grabbed a black leather jacket to go over her low-cut, blousy, gold knit top cinched at the waist by a wide black leather belt. Finally, she made it down the staircase to the Great Room.

"It's about time," Allisa said smiling. "Sure you're ready now?"

"Do you think I look okay?"

"Of course, *you* do, but that's not the question you should ask. The real question is will any of the guys look good enough to suit your tastes?"

"Are you insinuating I'm fussy?" Rocki asked, displaying her most sincere look.

"Oh my God! Seriously? You're so discriminatingly finicky, I really question if you'll ever find anyone who meets your standards. But let's go. I'm willing to give it a shot tonight."

"You are so reassuring, Allisa. Sometimes, I wonder why we even bother looking." Rocki set the house alarm and they finally headed out to Allisa's brand-new Camaro.

"We bother, because if we just sit here in your house all night, no *Knight in Shining Armor* is going to drive up into your driveway, walk up to your door and ring the doorbell. And then ask you to marry him. That's why."

"Really? What do you think the odds of that happening are?"

"Oh about, one in a million, probably."

"And what, pray tell, do you think the odds are we will find *Mr. Right* at the fabulous Redstone's bar tonight?" Rocki asked over the roof of the car as she got in.

Allisa started the engine. "More than one in a million because *some* men will be at Redstone's. And there are no men at your house, so the odds will at least be in our favor at the bar. Besides, where else can we meet eligible men?" She scrolled down her cell phone's music playlist to one of their signature songs—*I Will Survive*—and cranked up the volume on the stereo. They both sang along to the words as she backed out of the driveway.

Twenty minutes later, they arrived at Redstone's and valet parked the car. Allisa and Rocki could feel the vibrations of the music before they even walked through the entrance doors. Music was their thing. It calmed them and made them forget about everything else except the way the rhythm made them want to move their bodies in sensual unison with each beat.

They found seats at the bar and ordered glasses of Beringer's White Zinfandel wine. Each scanned the crowd to look over the prospects for the evening. It wasn't uncommon for neither one of them to find even one man who looked interesting to them. It seemed tonight wouldn't be any different, but the night was still young and there was no telling who may walk through the doors as the evening progressed. There was always a chance, slight though it may be and they each only needed one good man.

The question they kept asking themselves was where could they find one?

Rocki dejectedly looked at the sorry loser men surrounding them and felt like her goal was becoming more hopeless as each year passed by. She'd been divorced for three years now. Her ex had been restless for the last few years of their marriage. She'd known that, yes, but she thought he would get over his misguided notion that he was missing out on something. He ultimately came to the conclusion he couldn't find it while staying married to her. So, the week after their daughter left for college, he packed his stuff and left.

Rocki thought her life had surely ended that day, but she still had two children who loved her and brought happiness to her life. She liked being married, having someone to come home to and someone to do things with. Their sex life had always been good. Filled with passion. She really missed the sex. He was probably out having sex right now, with whomever he wanted to, which totally pissed her off. She, on the other hand, hadn't had sex since he'd left. Her friends told her to buy sex toys to relieve the sexual tension, but she wanted a live warm body to hold onto while she was having an orgasm, so she hadn't taken them up on their suggestions.

A couple, just about her and Allisa's age, sat down on stools next to Rocki.

She couldn't help but overhear bits and pieces of their conversation. One statement totally caught her attention. They had met on an internet dating service. Wow!

The couple got up to make their way to the dance floor.

"Allisa, I just overheard them saying they met on an internet dating service."

"Really. I heard some women at work talking about internet dating. Some have had bad luck and some have met good people," Allisa stated.

"It seems scary. How do you know if they are predators or stalkers or who knows?" Rocki asked.

"How do you know these guys here aren't predators or stalkers? You don't."

"I guess you're right. Should we just go home right now and maybe hibernate for the rest of our lives? Not take any chances because we might get hurt?" Rocki stared hopelessly at the dance floor.

"Whatever!" Allisa rolled her eyes. "From what I heard about internet dating, it does all the work for you as far as matching your likes and dislikes, religious beliefs, political views, etc. You can even look for an educated man with a great career and income. You certainly can't do that here by just looking at them. I think it would be a lot easier than this."

"Are you saying you want to try it?"

Allisa shrugged. "I don't know. It's scary, but so is this and we don't seem to be getting anywhere this way."

"You've got a point there." Rocki watched a man approach them.

"Would you beautiful ladies like to dance with me and my friend?" the man asked.

Rocki looked him over and really didn't see anything she liked, but answered, "And where's your friend?"

"I'll get him and be right back," he said and left.

A couple of minutes later, he walked back up with an older, grungy-looking bald man who reeked of cigarettes and alcohol.

He stood seemingly waiting for a response from her. "So do you ladies want to dance with me and my friend?" he asked again.

Rocki stared him directly in the eye and gave him her response, "I don't think so. Actually, there isn't a chance in Hell, we will be dancing with you *or* your friend."

He stared at her in disbelief, as if she hadn't actually just said what she'd said to him.

Rocki didn't flinch but instead held her stare.

He nodded, turned, motioned to his friend and left.

Allisa stared at Rocki in her own disbelief at what she'd just heard. "Oh, my God! I can't believe you just said that to them!"

"Were you going to dance with his friend?" Rocki asked straight-faced.

"Hell, no!"

"Okay then. Neither was I. I figured if he had the gall to think either of us would, he got no more than he deserved."

Both Rocki and Allisa broke out in uncontrollable laughter and had to hold on to the bar counter, so they wouldn't fall off their bar stools.

Needless to say, no one else approached them the rest of the night and they were perfectly all right with that. They talked, laughed, and danced to their favorite songs with each other until the band quit playing for the evening. *Who knows?* Maybe the men at Redstone's thought they were a couple, but they didn't care because there wasn't even one man in the whole bar that interested either of them.

They'd had enough fun by midnight for one evening, so they headed outside to pick up the Camaro at the valet stand. The convertible top was down in minutes, and their long hair was quickly put into ponytails. Allisa scrolled down her cell phone playlist to the most appropriate song for their ride home, *Holding out for a Hero,* and cranked up the volume. They sang along to the song as loud as they could.

# CHAPTER 2

⁊

After attending the late service at church, the next morning, Rocki met Allisa at Mystic Lake Casino to partake of the well-known and delicious food buffet. You could have breakfast or dinner, but the best way to partake of the massive food display was to try a little bit of everything. This was Rocki's plan and she would be full the rest of the day, which meant she wouldn't have to make dinner tonight.

Seated at the table with their plates full, they scanned the restaurant for eligible men.

"Do you see anyone who interests you?" Rocki asked Allisa.

"Not a one," Allisa answered. "How about you?"

"Not a single one, either."

"I'm thinking we should check out the internet dating sites. What do you think? Are you game to give it a shot?" Allisa suggested.

"But we don't know anything about internet dating. How do we know which ones are legit?"

"I've heard Life Match commercials on TV, so they should be legit. There's also a Christian one, Christian Couples. I think it's based on Christianity and finding a partner who has the same religious beliefs as you do, which according to the commercial…makes for a better marriage, of course."

"How about you stop over after we're done here and we can see what we can find as far as internet dating sites," Rocki suggested.

"I'm game, let's give it a shot, and get into the internet dating game."

Rocki and Allisa finished eating and dropped a couple dollars in the slot machines. Left the casino none the richer and headed to Rocki's house.

In the Great Room, they both sat down on the couch with laptops in hand, and made themselves comfortable. The laptops were powered up and soon, they were checking out various internet dating sites.

"I'm going to take a look at what Christian Couples has to offer." Allisa typed in her requirements for the man of her dreams and hit enter. There were thirty matches. "Hey, I got thirty men to check out!"

"Didn't you have to sign up and pay first?" Rocki asked after she got to the site.

"No, just put in what you are looking for and see what happens."

"Okay, here goes nothing." Rocki quickly filled in what she was looking for in the man of her dreams. "Hey, I have thirty, too." She read one bio with interest. "Wow, this guy is hot! Look at him!"

Allisa leaned over to take a look at Rocki's screen. "Yes, he is. Do you think you want him, because if you don't, I'll take him!"

"Whoa, I'm not even signed up yet. Check out your own." Rocki laughed. "Hey, you know this is fun, way more fun than the bar, that's for sure."

"I have to agree one hundred percent."

Rocki proceeded to check out the next man. "This guy looks good, too. Do you think we should sign up? Because we can't email them unless we're signed up."

"Let's check out Life Match first and see what they have available in men, maybe they'll have even better matches for us." Allisa smiled.

"I'm going to finish looking at these matches first."

"Mine all look like potential keepers. Yours probably will, too. I'm going to check out the Life Match site." Allisa typed in the website address.

Rocki leaned over to see if Allisa had any matches up yet. "You're right, they all look like good matches. He looks good."

"They're all looking good. Maybe we should sign up for both sites?" Allisa questioned.

"Well, we could but maybe we should just try one first and see what happens and if it doesn't work out, we can use the other site as a back-up plan." Rocki couldn't help smiling.

"Okay, which one do you want to try first? The good boys or the bad boys?"

"What?" Rocki asked.

"The good old church boys or the rebel type bad boys?" Allisa questioned.

"Oh, I got it. I think we should do the bad boys first, so Life Match it is." Rocki clicked on the sign-up page and started filling in her information.

"I think you're right. So, we're actually doing this?" Allisa asked, even though she could see Rocki filling out the sign-up sheet. "Okay." She clicked the box for the sign-up page on her laptop, too. "We need to load a picture or pictures. What picture should I use?"

"I'm going to use a headshot I have from the sexy photo shoot I had done a few years back." Rocki began searching in her photo library for the picture and maybe a couple others to use.

"Oh, that's right you had them taken, so you could give him a framed photo for his birthday, but then he left. Did you ever give him one?" Allisa asked.

"No. There certainly wasn't any point at the time. But it's a nice picture, so what the heck? Might as well put it to some use."

"I don't have a sexy one like that but I had a professional picture taken last year for work. I can use that one." Allisa began going through her photo file.

"How about one with my kids? Maybe a Christmas one taken by the Christmas tree?" Rocki asked.

"Christmas pictures should work." Allisa continued browsing

through her pictures until she found the professional headshot. She continued on looking for one of her Christmas pictures.

Rocki got up, grabbed her purse, and took out a credit card to pay the fee for using the dating website. Eagerly, she entered her card number. "I'm excited about this new adventure. It could be the start of something great for both of us. We could ultimately meet the loves of our lives. This is a huge monumental step for us."

"Okay, okay. Let's not start celebrating until we meet Mr. Right. You do realize there will be a whole lot of Mr. Wrongs before we get to Mr. Right?" Allisa's expression became serious.

"Sure. But we have to start somewhere. Right?" Rocki countered.

"What should I use for my screen name?" Alli focused on her laptop screen.

"I don't know, I'm stuck on that one myself," Rocki stated.

"I'm thinking maybe something with my name in it. AlliCat, AllOf-Lisa, MonaLisa, AlliLove?"

"Those are great."

"I'm liking AlliCat," Allisa said.

"How about WildRock? LadyLikesRock, LikeARock, RockFullOf-Life, LoveRocks for me? Like any of those?" Rocki asked.

"I like LoveRocks."

"Good choice, I like that one best, too." Rocki smiled.

Rocki and Allisa entered their screen names into the computer program.

"Okay, here goes. I'm typing an email introduction to my first match," Allisa said matter-of-factly.

"Me, too. Here goes nothing."

"Are you going to respond to all of them?" Allisa asked as she kept on typing.

"I think I'm going to simply type a short blurb about myself and then copy and paste it in the next one. That way, it will go much faster and then it will allow me to get through all of them quickly." Rocki felt very proud of herself since she'd come up with such an efficient way of dealing with this whole internet dating process.

"That's a great idea! I'm going to do that, too. Then we can wait for our responses to come back. Do you think we'll get any back right away?" Allisa asked.

"I noticed it states on their profiles the last time they were on the site. Some said online now or within 24 hours, so we'll see. I think it really depends on when they access their account."

"That makes sense," Allisa said.

"Do you think we could actually have dates for tonight?" Rocki eagerly asked as she was hoping to get started meeting these men who were potential matches.

"I'm not sure how fast it works. Do you think we should email a few times first or just meet them right away?" Allisa asked.

"I don't want to waste their time or mine emailing," Rocki replied, as she continued to send emails. "It basically depends on whether during the first face to face meeting either it clicks or it doesn't. So, I think I want to meet them as soon as possible."

"Of course, we need to keep in mind safety is important so we should probably stick to public places such as coffee shops or restaurants for first meetings."

"Yes, that's a good plan. So, if we meet at a restaurant, who buys?" Rocki asked.

"I don't know, what do you think is appropriate?" Allisa asked.

"I think if a couple of hours of conversation with me aren't worth a dinner, then there won't be a second date. I think I'm definitely worth it."

"I agree." Allisa nodded. "If he can't spring for dinner, he's not the guy for me. But we'll have to see, sometimes just meeting for a glass of wine might be okay."

"Maybe, we'll have to see," Rocki said.

"Do you think we need to keep a file system going on these men? I think we'll need to print out their profile before the dates, so we can brush up on their likes and dislikes, hobbies, jobs, children, etc."

"Wow, you're right. I think we'll need to do print outs before the dates." Rocki powered down her laptop. "It will almost be like a job where you need to know everything about your product and everything about who you're selling your product to."

"I've got some errands to run, so I'm going to take off," Allisa said. "I'll call you later when I get home and let you know the status on my returned emails from my maybe perfect men."

"Okay, I won't check mine till you call and let me know you're home. Deal?" Rocki offered.

"Deal." Allisa left to take care of her errands, as they would take up a couple of hours. That way she wouldn't be tempted to check her emails too soon.

# CHAPTER 3

*R*ocki walked out through her patio door to the massive cedar deck overlooking Prior Lake. The snow was finally gone, the trees were budding as the tulips, iris and tiger lilies were beginning to bloom, also. This was a beautiful time of the year and she always loved spring because it meant new beginnings for nature. Whatever was hibernating almost as if it were dead would come to life again after bearing the brunt of a brutally cold and long winter.

She also felt like this was her time to come back to life after her devastating divorce. Life had been brutal during the divorce proceedings that lasted nearly two years. In fact, she'd felt as if she'd died, well at the very least a part of her had died, that she was sure of. The pain was extremely overwhelming causing her to crash and burn for a short time. So, when it was over, she decided it was best to put everything behind her, then move on to bigger and better things. She wasn't moving from her executive home on the lake even though it held many bitter memories. No, that was out of the question as far as she was concerned. It was her dream house and she was keeping it. And he would pay for it, since he had chosen to leave.

Spring was definitely in the air, plus it was the beginning of a new year which was definitely going to be the beginning of a new life for her. She walked down the steps leading to the lake. The sky was a vivid blue with no clouds in sight. The dark blue water of the lake appeared so still, like it resembled glass. It was too early in the season for boats to be out on the lake, since most were probably still in storage. But in a few weeks, the water would be filled with boats and jet skis.

Rocki sat down on the stone wall near the lakeshore. This was her favorite spot, so serene and quiet, a welcoming place to be alone with your thoughts. She wanted a new beginning, Hell, she deserved a new beginning. He'd been foolish and given up the best thing to ever happen to him—meaning her. Somewhere out there, were other men and she was determined to find a man with whom she could begin a new life. A new journey of love and adventure. She was open to trying different things at this stage in her life. With her hands folded, she whispered a silent prayer to God to help her find Mr. Right, as she wasn't sure she would make the right choice without God's help.

A couple of hours later, Rocki's phone rang.

"I'm home, so what do you say, should we check our emails?" Allisa asked. "Or did you already sneak a peek?"

"Nope, no peeking. Truthfully, I'm kind of scared to look. What if no one answered our emails?"

"Rocki, we're hot! Of course, they'll answer our emails. Plus, we're smart."

"I hope so," Rocki answered sitting down at the kitchen table with her laptop and entering her password.

"I have three emails!" Allisa exclaimed.

"Well, open them! What do they say?" Rocki asked.

"I'm getting there. Did you get any?" Allisa asked.

Rocki held her breath while she opened Life Match. "Oh my God, I have four emails!"

"Yes!" Allisa cheered. "I have one who wants to meet tonight. His codename is *SurferJoe*. His bio sounds good, exactly what I'm looking for. I am going to go for it and meet him at Applebee's."

"I have one who wants to meet tonight, too. Should we go to the same place? That way we can check out each other's dates."

"Sure, then we'll feel safe, too."

"His codename is *Mr.Wrong*. Can you believe it?" Rocki asked.

"Well, it is a screen name after all. How does his bio sound?" Allisa asked.

"Like a total Casanova bad boy! He has a Harley, boat, Corvette, jet skis, travels all over, oh and his body is to die for. He must have a six-pack, but the picture doesn't show his face. I'm not meeting him until I can see his face," Rocki stated matter-of-factly.

"Are you sure? It might be fun anyway," Allisa prompted.

"You know what…he wasn't one of the ones I sent emails to earlier. He emailed me."

"Wow, that means he's interested in you because he made the first move. If you don't want to meet him tonight, send him a reply asking for a picture," Allisa said.

"I can do that, I suppose. He signed it—Nick."

"I just sent *SurferJoe* a reply and he answered already. He'll meet me at Applebee's."

"I just got another one from a *KnightInShiningArmor*. He wants to meet. Let me see if tonight works for him," Rocki said as she typed her reply and sent it.

"It's only four o'clock, so you still have time. I'm going to send replies to the other three guys to try and set up a date for next week. Maybe I can have a date each night! Even when I was younger, I never did that. I think I like this new dating!"

"He replied already! He will meet me tonight at Applebee's. Do you think we can get tables close to each other?" Rocki asked.

"Probably unless they are packed, which I doubt since it's Sunday," Allisa stated. "So does this guy sound like a keeper?"

"He looks good and his bio sounds good, so we'll just wait to see," Rocki replied. "I'm going to get going. Have to find something to wear. Oh my God! I have no idea what to wear!"

"You have a whole closet full of clothes, so just pick something. Let's meet at Applebee's at six thirty. Okay?" Allisa asked.

"See you there." Rocki ended the call and practically ran up the steps to her bedroom.

Rocki stood, staring at her closet. She absolutely had nothing to wear on a date with a hot guy. What she wore to the bar on Saturday night was about the only thing she had that looked hot. She was definitely going clothes shopping after work tomorrow night. After all, this was her new beginning and she wanted to look her best. Her highly conservative work wardrobe would not do at all. Rocki quickly dressed but took extra time with her makeup, wanting to look her best for this man who could possibly be the, *Love of her Life.*

~

AT SIX THIRTY, Rocki pulled into the parking lot at Applebee's.

Minutes later, Allisa pulled in and parked.

They walked up to the front of the restaurant and sat down on the park bench to wait for the men.

"I'm nervous," Rocki admitted.

"Me, too, but it'll be fun." Allisa snickered. "Simply look at it like we're interviewing the men to see if they meet our requirements for that special man, we want to spend the rest of our lives with."

"You know I never thought of it like that, but you're totally right. We'll be interviewing them, while they're probably busy checking us out physically to see if we turn them on. For most men, turning them on isn't tough."

"You're so right! It's harder for women," Allisa said as she eyed a man approaching them, who was most likely her date for dinner.

"Alli?" he asked as he approached her.

Allisa stood up and shook his hand. "Yes, and you are Joe?"

"Yes," he said and motioned her towards the door.

Allisa walked into Applebee's with her date, Joe.

This left Rocki on the bench alone. It wasn't quite seven yet, so she sat patiently waiting.

Minutes later, a man walked towards her.

"Rocki?" Terry Knight asked.

"Yes," Rocki said and stood to shake his outstretched hand. She walked into the restaurant through the door he held open. They were seated a couple of booths down from Allisa and her date.

Rocki and Terry talked while eating dinner. They shared stories about themselves, talked about their children and the highlights of their lives. Rocki assumed Allisa and Joe were probably having a similar conversation. About nine o'clock, she saw Allisa and Joe stand up to leave. She was ready to leave, too. "I think I should get going. Tomorrow's a work day."

Terry and Rocki walked out to their cars five minutes later.

"Would you like to go out again?" Terry asked.

Rocki froze. What did one to say to that question? She hadn't felt an instant attraction, but she wasn't sure how it worked. Did you feel it right away? Terry was a likeable guy and good looking.

He stood waiting for her answer.

"That would be nice. Just send me an email."

"I will. Thanks for a nice evening," Terry said and leaned towards her for a hug. Then he walked to his car.

Rocki got into her car and reached into her purse for her cell. She saw there already was a voicemail from Allisa. She started the car, pressed the phone button, and called her.

"So how did it go? Are you in love?" Allisa asked laughing.

"Don't think so, how about you?" Rocki responded.

"Oh well, one down and many, many more to go. This was just our test run," Allisa stated emphatically. "It's getting late, so I'll call you tomorrow. I'm going to try and set up a date for tomorrow night when I get home."

"Okay, talk to you tomorrow. Actually, I'll email you from work."

Rocki turned on her computer immediately after arriving home. She wanted to see if *Mr.Wrong* sent her a picture. For some odd reason, he really intrigued her, and maybe for all the wrong reasons. After all, he probably actually was a *bad boy* and she certainly didn't need a *bad boy*, so why did she think she wanted one?

# CHAPTER 4

*D*ominick Taggart had at least fifty emails to answer tonight. Life Match dating site was proving to be far more advantageous to his Master's Thesis than he'd ever expected. He never thought it would be this easy to gather information about internet dating. Having dual profiles might get a bit tricky but then again, he wasn't actually dating to find a life match, he was doing research. He certainly wouldn't let his heart become too involved, or so he tried to convince himself. He already doubted the soundness of the whole idea after looking at the pictures and profiles of these women. They were *hot* and they were intelligent women. Hopefully, they would not be able to see through his profiles to his real reason for being on Life Match.

Interestingly enough, there were a number of women who didn't seem to care if his picture showed his face or not. Did that mean they weren't into looks? Or maybe they weren't paying attention and sent out a mass email to all their matches. On the other hand, there were a number of women who didn't want to proceed without a picture. He had a couple of other pictures he was prepared to add to his profile, only they were photos of him from the distance so it was hard to see his face. The initial one he posted was on a boat where he was wearing dark sunglasses with a baseball hat and the lighting was deliberately dark. Tonight, he would post others, one skiing in Vail, one on his Harley, one in his Corvette and one scuba diving. None had a clear view of his face.

Now it was time to type up another mass email, to all those who wanted a better picture. He would include in the email something stating he was only looking for a good time. It would be blunt and to the point, no sugar coatings insinuating he may want a life partner. Then of course, if he found the right woman, he would certainly want to spend much more time with her.

It read:

*As for the picture, it's the best one I have and besides, I don't think you want me to think you are only into looks and want a HOT guy. I'm a good person, great looking—you will have to take my word on that—fun to be with, love to have a good time and not sure I would be any good at a long-term relationship. But then again, who knows, if I come across the right person, I might take the big step. In the meantime, I am looking to have fun and will definitely show you a good time. After all, we are all adults here and free to come and go as we please.*

*If you pass on going out with me, you will never know what pleasures could've been yours simply for the asking. I recently posted additional pictures for your viewing pleasure.*

*Mr.Wrong*

*LoveRocks'* email caught his eye. Of course, she requested a picture. He was intrigued by her story. It seemed very sincere, but who knew better than him, how deceiving a person's profile could be. Look at his. He totally wanted to meet her, but she declined due to the vague pictures.

*LoveRocks,*

*I recently loaded a couple more pictures and hope we can set up a meeting. I look forward to seeing you in person.*

*Mr.Wrong*

He searched for his pictures, loaded them into his profile, and then began sending his mass email response to all the lucky ladies who were part of the research project for his thesis. One at a time. Since he was curious about *LoveRocks*, he sent hers first.

After finishing his return emails, he searched for any new matches and found a few more of interest then sent them his first mass email.

Now to move on to *Mr.Right*. First, he needed to set up the profile and of course, use a different email, name and address. He was tempted to use his real name for *Mr.Right* since he used Nick Sager, a fictitious name for *Mr.Wrong*. No, he couldn't take the chance, so he would use another fictitious name. Dom Darulo would work for *Mr.Right*.

He sent out another mass email, but this one was different, more the good guy type. And he intended on sending it to all the same women. It took a little bit of time, but finally he had an email he was satisfied with.

*I'm one of the last good guys out here. I'm looking for a committed long-term relationship with the woman of my dreams. I know she's out there, we just have to meet first. I'm sincere, know how to treat a lady, and I am looking for love.*

*Mr.Right*

He immediately began sending the emails out one by one again. After they were all sent, he checked through his new emails, looking for one in particular—*LoveRocks*. It was late though and disappointingly, it wasn't there. Why was he so interested in this one anyway? He'd never cared enough about any of the women in his life to marry them. He certainly had plenty of relationships during the years and they'd lasted more than a couple of years at a time. When the women would push for marriage and he couldn't make the commitment, they moved on and ultimately, he moved on to the next woman. So, this was how his very predictable past had gone.

He'd always felt lucky, in a way, that his college sweetheart kept the baby they'd conceived together on their gradation night. He'd broken up with her a few weeks later, so he didn't find out about the baby until five years later when he'd contacted her. He'd sowed his wild oats and was finally ready to settle down at that point in his life. So, he married her and he'd taken his role seriously as a husband and parent, making room in his life for his one and only child, Ryder Taggert. After his wife's untimely death years ago, his daughter, Ryder was the only woman in his life who he had a lifelong commitment to.

So far, anyway.

He basically didn't see it changing at this point in his life, but then again in recent years, he simply hadn't felt like he'd met the right person, at least not yet, to take a chance on again. Someone whose face he wanted to see every morning for the rest of his life. His friends always told him there was someone out there for him, he just had to keep looking. His safeguard had always been to have a relationship with someone he liked, but also someone he knew he could live without. This would take him off the market for a few years at a time. And who knows? Maybe during that time, he missed out on possibly meeting that one special person, because when he was in a relationship, he was committed to that person and he no longer was looking.

The research project totally intrigued him because he found it hard to believe anyone could actually find their special person on an online dating service. But hard as it may have seemed to meet someone special online, the internet dating services produced large numbers of marriages. The matching process itself was impressive though and matched key factors of relationships such as religion, politics, smoking, drinking, hobbies, ages, ethnicity, goals and desires for a potential mate.

Unfortunately, he'd obviously given up on love, which was the reason he quit looking after his last relationship ended over a year ago. He simply didn't want to look anymore if she wasn't out there. Instead, it was best to simply have a good time with the women he met. Which was exactly what he was doing. In a way, he was basically like *Mr.Wrong* which would make it easy to play the part. It wouldn't even take much acting on his part, because he was already living it every day of his life.

Now, as far as his role of being *Mr.Right*, it would be a little bit tougher. Deep down, he wanted to be the guy who could find that special woman, actually propose, and go through with the wedding. A part of him really was *that* guy. This would be a great opportunity to play the role of *Mr.Right*. And a way for him to meet a lot of women to see if there was even one who stood a chance of being *the one* who could even slightly tempt him to consider spending the rest of his life waking up next to.

Strange thing was he kept thinking about *LoveRocks* and was literally waiting for her email.

# CHAPTER 5

*R*ocki's computer couldn't power up fast enough for her needs. Finally, Life Match's home page appeared on her screen. She quickly clicked on emails. There were ten emails and yes, one was from *Mr.Wrong*! She couldn't believe the gall of his forthright statements. He basically said he was a stud and only looking for a good time! He signed it Nick Sager. Even his name fit the profile and sounded like a bad boy's name. Definitely wasn't what she was looking for. But it actually did sound fun. What could she possibly be thinking? He could be fun? Hell, she'd been married for twenty-four years and yes, her sad excuse for a husband had ditched her right when the kids were getting ready to plan their big twenty-fifth wedding anniversary party. There was no question in her mind that he was out having *fun*, so maybe she should, too.

She'd been a good wife, never cheated, never even thought about cheating, and hadn't ever given other men the eye. No, she'd done it all by the book and she'd lost the game. She wasn't so sure she wanted to get married again, at least not right away, anyway. She hadn't done much dating when she was young. Since she'd met her husband in college and married shortly afterwards, he was the only man she'd had sex with all these years. To be truthful, she wasn't sure she could actually have sex with another man. It would just plain feel awkward. First, she'd have to take off her clothes and she wasn't so sure she could do it. Not that she was ashamed of her body, quite the contrary. She was in great shape, thanks to a great metabolism, yoga classes, and tennis. But being naked in front of a man, would be a totally different thing. A man would stare at your naked body, slowly and precisely, taking in every inch of bare skin and some men could even commit that picture to memory. At least, that's what she'd heard. Damn those men with photographic memories. Lord only knew what was going on in their minds at that moment, but she was pretty sure it had to do with having sex every way imaginable.

Because of this fact, she wasn't even sure why she'd considered the whole internet dating process in the first place. She'd better just focus on finding one man to spend the rest of her life with. That way, she would only have to take her clothes off in front of one more man and only have sex with him. There basically wasn't any way she was cut out to have sex with multiple men. No way. It simply wasn't going to happen. And now after considering all this, every time she went out with a new man on Life Match, one of the first things she would consider after meeting him was—*Could she have sex with him?* Maybe just staying home and being alone wasn't such a bad idea after all. Why had she let Allisa talk her into this whole internet dating thing? But deep down, she knew the reason. She was lonely.

She needed to focus on the task at hand. Answering *Mr.Wrong's* email.

*Nick,*

*Thanks for your interest in meeting me, but I don't think you are what I am looking for. Maybe you should reread my profile, because it says I'm looking for a committed one on one relationship which definitely is not what you are looking for. You have the bad boy persona down to a tee though, so I am sure you'll easily be able to find women who are looking for the same thing. I wish you the best in your search.*

*LoveRocks*

Good. Now that was done. So why was she actually feeling a little sad, knowing she wouldn't hear from him again?

Moving forward, the next email was from *SunSetter*, he looked good in his photos and apparently liked the water and boating. The important things matched, so she sent him a reply, asking if he wanted to meet her tomorrow night.

Next one was from *GuyForYou*. He was her age, nice looking and they had a lot in common. So how did one work this process to get a date for tomorrow night? She basically would have to ask multiple matches, since everyone had different schedules and things going on in their lives. She sent him a reply asking if he was free Monday or Tuesday night.

Next one was from *LoveToLoveYou*. Really! Their profile names were way too much. He was ten years younger than her. What could he possibly be thinking? There was no way she would go out with someone so young! She sent him a reply stating there was way too much of an age gap.

Next one was from *Retired*. This one was just as bad, he was ten years older than her and from the pictures, he looked like he could be her dad. No, this definitely wouldn't work either. He stated he was set for life financially and his match would be, also. It didn't matter how much money he had, because there wasn't any way she could ever have sex with him. She sent him an email stating she was looking for someone closer to her age.

Next one was from *Traveler*. He appeared to be nice looking and was an airline pilot who still loved to travel, even though he'd been all over the world. She liked his profile and even thought to herself, *I think I could have sex with this guy*. She sent him an email asking if he would like to meet and to let her know what his schedule was for next week.

Next one was from *HarleyGuy*. He was good looking in that tough guy style. Although, looks could be deceiving because his occupation was a lawyer. She wondered how she would look all decked out in leathers. Not too bad probably. Their profiles had a lot in common, so what the heck? She would give it a shot. She sent him an email, asking if he wanted to meet on Wednesday.

Next one was from *Jazzman*. Wow, a musician. He played Jazz-

Blues music and sang. She loved Blues music. They matched on most things, but on some, they didn't. On this one she didn't really care, she was intrigued by the music part and wanted to meet him. Hopefully, she would get to see him perform, too. She sent him an email and asked if he'd like to meet this coming week some time.

Next one was from *Mr.Right*. There was no picture, but stated you could request one. Their profiles matched perfectly and they were about the same ages. He was a writer, so maybe he wasn't being cocky with his profile name, maybe it was simply a play on words. She sent an email requesting a picture.

There were still two from earlier in the day to look at.

One was from *DealBreaker*. He wasn't great looking and his deal breaker was if you were so into looks you couldn't give an average guy with a big heart a chance, you lost out. For a moment, she wondered if maybe the picture wasn't his at all. Oh, what the heck, she could have a cup of coffee with him. She sent him an email asking if he wanted to meet for coffee sometime next week.

Finally, the last one and it was from *Romeo*. He was fifteen years younger than her and she didn't even feel like he deserved a return email. All his email said was, "You're one hot babe!" Her reply simply said, "Thanks, but no thanks."

With all her emails sent out, she closed out of Life Match. She'd had enough of the whole dating thing for one day. After all, she did have to go to work at the Prior Lake Newspaper in the morning. She looked at the clock and saw it was eleven. Definitely time to get ready for bed and pick out something to wear tomorrow. She couldn't wait to tell the girls at work about her weekend. They probably wouldn't believe it. She would need proof.

She powered the laptop back up and signed back in to Life Match. She'd totally forgot to print off their profiles with pictures which she needed for her file folder to keep track of who she'd emailed back and was waiting for their response and who she'd sent out emails to. Once on the site, she clicked on each one of the emails she'd responded to tonight and clicked print. She even printed the ones she'd declined. The girls at work were going to get a kick out of this whole thing tomorrow. They'd actually suggested she give internet dating a try a couple of years ago, after her divorce.

Finally, about midnight, she climbed into bed. It had been quite a day. She closed her eyes but the profile picture - make that the vague profile pictures of *Mr.Wrong* - kept popping into her head. Damn! He definitely was the wrong guy for her, but hey wasn't that what dreams were for? There, you could be with whoever you wanted. . .be it *Mr.Wrong* or *Mr.Right*.

# CHAPTER 6

The day came in as a bright shiny Monday morning, with the sun streaming through Dominick's home office windows and the patio doors, leading to the deck on his multi-million-dollar house on Prior Lake. His friends always gave him crap for buying a house on Prior Lake when he could've just as easily bought one on Lake Minnetonka. There wasn't anything wrong with Lake Minnetonka, it was just too big for his liking. Prior Lake just seemed so much quainter and yes, the lake was smaller but big enough for him. Mostly, he liked the still somewhat small town feel it had in its old downtown area. Plus, there were plenty of stores and restaurants within minutes, whereas depending on which part of Lake Minnetonka you were on, it could be 20-30 minutes to get to shopping and eating establishments.

He'd already stopped at the little downtown bakery to have a Danish and a cup of coffee while reading the Prior Lake local newspaper. He liked to read it to get the local news firsthand. The photographer who took the spring flower pictures hanging on the walls of the bakery had done an excellent job. Now back at home, he sat down at his desk to get to work.

First thing was to sign into Life Match and see what he had for responses to his emails sent from *Mr.Wrong* and then the ones sent from *Mr.Right*. He had two piles of file folders on his desk to keep the print outs of the emails he'd sent and the ones he'd received.

The file folder for *LoveRocks* was on the top of both files. He opened the folder to look at the picture of her he'd printed out the night before. Unfortunately, she was exactly what he was looking for in a woman. Everything matched. Too bad, he hadn't met her outside of this dating research project because simply looking at her picture turned him on. He was really looking forward to meeting her.

*LoveRocks* was the first email he looked for in the list of many. Actually, there were a hundred in total, meaning fifty had responded to his email from *Mr.Wrong* and another fifty were from his *Mr.Right* emails. He was in the *Mr.Wrong* account and hers was the top one because she'd responded last. He opened up the email, read it, and laughed. This woman had spunk. She'd given it back to him, that's for sure. He liked that and now, he wanted to meet her even more. The tactic of this project was to keep after these women to see how long it would take them to say '*Yes*' to *Mr.Wrong*.

*LoveRocks,*

*I understand your thinking regarding 'Bad Boys' is highly negative, but let's get one thing straight first, no one gets married on the second date. So, you can rest assured on a first date nothing bad will happen to you, in fact you'll be perfectly safe. I'll be at Starbucks next to the Burnsville Center after work tomorrow at five thirty waiting for you.*

*Nick*

What were the odds she would show up after an email like that? Extremely slim. But he was willing to bet on her curiosity getting the best of her. His gut told him she would show up. Then he would go from there. After meeting her in person, he would know if his plan would work. That is if she looked anything like her picture. He hoped she did. Now though, he wasn't sure he stood a chance of *not* getting personally involved in this whole research project. At least not with her. Hell, he already wanted her. This wasn't good. But at least, she was the only one he'd had this reaction to.

Dominick typed up another mass email to send back to the others.

He would use it and then add a line or two to the bottom, depending on what they'd said in their replies.

He sent off replies to them setting up meetings for coffee in the morning, lunch, afternoon coffee, dinner, and drinks later in the evening. Granted, some would have to be rearranged, so his schedule probably wouldn't be that full. He had a large calendar he'd picked up at Office Max, to write down all the appointments on. They would of course, be put into his cell phone, but the calendar would allow him to see all of them at once, if needed.

The profile names women chose were incredibly interesting. After doing some calculating, he decided on only four a day.

His first response was to *LadyInWaiting* for coffee before work on Tuesday, *ScarletLady_* for lunch on Tuesday, and *GypsyWoman* for dinner at seven on Tuesday. Then of course, he would meet *LoveRocks* for coffee after work on Tuesday.

Moving on to Wednesday, he scheduled *HarleyGal* for coffee about nine, *SusyQ* for lunch, *LadyInRed* for early dinner at five thirty, and *SexyLady* for drinks at nine.

Then moving on to Thursday, *LakerGal* for morning coffee. *SkiBum* for lunch, *TravelBug* for a drink after work, and *LadyMadonna* for dinner at seven thirty.

On Friday, *MarathonRunner* for morning coffee, *DancingQueen* for lunch, *RomanticOne* for early dinner and *RoseLady* for drinks at nine.

This could take a while, since by Friday, he would only be through sixteen matches. It sounded tiring but this was his work for the thesis, so he needed to put the time in. They may not all be able to make it on the times he proposed. So, he may actually have some downtime which he would use to write down his notes after each meeting.

He got up to walk around and stretch. With it being noon already, he went to the kitchen to make a sandwich and salad. He turned on the news to see if anything important happened in the world this morning. And nothing had.

Now for Saturday, *FloridaGal* for early coffee, *YogaForLife* for lunch, *LadyGagaFan* for afternoon coffee or drinks. *LadyBoater* for dinner and maybe, he could catch up with *LoveRocks* later, so he was keeping that slot open just in case.

Sunday was all the further he intended to go for today. So *ChevyGal* for early coffee, *TopDown* for lunch, *RedRidingHood* for early dinner and *VampireQueen* for drinks later.

He'd already received about ten replies and they'd all agreed to his times. Must've really written an appealing bad boy profile. Well, everyone always said women liked the bad boys. In fact, they were drawn to them. Now, if only he could pull it off without any hitches. Good thing he'd been exactly that—a bad boy in high school and then again after college. Yes, he had the big bad Harley, the BMW convertible and the money—thanks to his dad. Oddly enough, the good guys could have all the toys, too. It basically depended on how you interpreted the crazy mixed sex signals encountered in the process of searching for your soul mate. In the meantime, both the bad boys and good guys just keep on looking until they find that special woman. Only the bad boys have a Hell of a good time with all the women they'd met in the meantime.

# CHAPTER 7

*T*oday had been by far, the best day she'd had at work in a long time. Her co-workers were ecstatic to hear she'd taken the plunge and signed up for Life Match. She repeatedly listened to how they'd all urged her to do it months and months ago. The file folders with each potential match made the rounds and they all gave their opinions as to who they thought was the best match for her. Of course, they all made the point of saying you can't tell by a picture and some nice words, you had to meet them face to face to see if there was any chemistry. They all emphatically agreed on the chemistry part. To Rocki, that part was a no brainer as far as she was concerned.

On her lunch break, she checked her Life Match inbox for emails. Her anticipation was running in high gear as the emails appeared. She felt relief when she saw one from *SunSetter*, although she wasn't sure why since it could very well be a decline to her invitation. But it wasn't, it was an acceptance email inviting her to dinner tonight at the Cheesecake Factory in Edina. She was ecstatic! Immediately, she sent an email accepting. Her clothes situation needed to be rectified quickly though. Her boss was more than accommodating and said she could leave at three, which would give her a couple of hours to do some quick shopping.

She opened the next email which was from *GuyForYou*, stating he would be more than happy to meet her tonight after work about seven for dinner. Crap! That would be her luck! She quickly sent a reply stating she had made other plans for the evening, but she could meet him on Tuesday if that worked.

*LoveToLoveYou* sent a reply stating, he understood, but yet he didn't understand. She was passing up a totally good guy but if she changed her mind to send him an email. Man, some guys just didn't know how to accept a polite decline.

And *Retired* sent a reply also! She had totally expected to not hear from him again. He also told her she was passing up the best match and to please email him when she had come to that realization. Really? Maybe a sugar coated NO, simply didn't cut it with internet dating.

No reply from *Traveler* or *HarleyGuy*. But it hadn't even been twenty-four hours yet, so she wasn't discounting them altogether.

*JazzMan* replied and wanted to meet her on Wednesday after work for a drink at Bonfire in Prior Lake. She sent an email accepting.

*DealBreaker* wanted to meet after work on Thursday for a coffee at Starbucks at the Village Mall. She sent an email accepting.

And believe it or not, *Romeo* sent an email stating that if she had a change of heart to please email him.

She couldn't believe her eyes when she saw an email from *Mr.Wrong*.

He actually had the gall to tell her she was to meet him on Tuesday after work at Starbucks at the Burnsville Center. In fact, it was more like an order—no, on second thought, more like a challenge than an invitation. She immediately sent a scathing reply.

*Nick,*

*So sorry to disappoint but I already have plans for the evening and even if I didn't, I would not be meeting you as we have nothing in common. Absolutely nothing. Ultimately, we would be a very bad match. And for the record, I have no intentions of ever meeting you.*

*LoveRocks*

Wow, that made her feel bad. She had never deliberately said scathing words to anyone. There was a lot to be said for beating around the bush. There was no future with Nick, so why bother and waste the time she could spend with other guys?

Her lunch was over and she needed to get back to work. She would hit the Burnsville Mall after work to look for clothes to make her look sexy and *hot*.

A couple of hours later, she was at the shopping center looking for dating clothes, if there even was such a thing. She managed to find a couple of sexy shirts, plus a pair of straight legged skin tight jeans, a new flowy sweater and some trendy spiked heels. Pleased with her purchases, she made her way home to change clothes.

She put on her new skin tight jeans and a slinky black top that hugged her breasts. On her wrists and temples, she dabbed on her newly acquired, *Bronze Goddess*, cologne. Lastly, she slipped on her new Jessica Simpson three-inch heels. She was ready. The Southdale Shopping Center was about thirty minutes away and she needed to get on the way, since it would definitely still be rush hour.

Rocki walked into Cheesecake Factory and didn't see *SunSetter*, whose name was Sonny. This was the awkward part of meeting someone in public when you've never actually met before.

A few minutes later, a man walked up to her and asked, "Rocki?"

"Yes," she answered.

"I'm Sonny. Let's get a table," he stated and walked over to the hostess desk.

They were both led by the hostess to be seated in a booth.

"I'm glad tonight worked out for you," Rocki said.

"Me, too. I'm glad to meet you," he replied.

"So, what do you like to do for fun?" Rocki asked for lack of a better question.

The conversation flowed well and they got to know each other better, ordered dinner and cheesecake, of course. After all, it was the Cheesecake Factory.

This had been another pleasant date and he seemed to be a likeable guy, but she didn't feel any chemistry at all. He would be a great friend though. Unfortunately, Rocki was positive that wasn't what he was looking for from her.

# CHAPTER 8

*D*ominick was shocked. *LoveRocks* turned him down scathingly…with class. Boy, did he have her pegged wrong. He had been absolutely positive she would accept. If she thought that was the end of him, she was wrong. It was only the beginning. Let the real game begin.

*LoveRocks,*

*I am disappointed to hear you have a previous engagement, but we can reschedule. I'd love to meet you Saturday night at nine at Redstone's in Eden Prairie. Wear something sexy. I'm anxious to see if you look as good as your picture. This time, I'm not taking no for an answer, so if you have plans cancel them. See you Saturday night.*

*Nick*

Now he just had to wait for her reply. He wondered how long she would hold out before agreeing to meet him. He hoped not too long, because he really wanted to see her in person.

The afternoon had flown by while he typed notes for his thesis' beginning, but he was almost finished. Just in time to change clothes and get cleaned up for his dinner tonight with his daughter, Ryder. She attended Gustavus College in St. Peter, about one hour away and was coming home to go shopping at the Mall of America, since she didn't have classes on Tuesday. When her mother and his wife, Anna, died about five years ago in a car accident, he and Ryder had become even closer. Anna had been the only love in his life. He'd owed her so much after rescuing him from his bad boy life after college of not caring about anything or anyone. He'd loved her with every breath of his body and there was now a huge void in his life. He was lonely, although, he would never admit it to anyone. That's why he decided to pick this project to write about. His curiosity had gotten the best of him and he actually wanted to know how this whole internet dating process worked.

Who knew, maybe if he saw any merit in it after his research, he might give it a try after the thesis was done and the book was written. He actually had been playing the bad boy to some extent already, dating women but not allowing them or himself to get close. Not getting involved allowed him to not have to think about making commitments to anyone. Having sex with random strangers hadn't appealed to him. It just wasn't the same as making love to his wife all those years. Unfortunately or fortunately, the shower had won out more times than he cared to think about. It also was far safer, medically speaking.

"Daddy, I'm home," Ryder said as she walked through the front door and up the staircase.

Dominick walked out of his master bedroom to embrace his daughter. "So how was your drive?"

"Oh, fine. I see you're ready. I need to change. I'll be down in fifteen minutes," Ryder said and walked into her bedroom to change into more appropriate clothes for the mall.

"Okay, see you downstairs," Dominick replied. "I thought we'd go to the Cheesecake Factory, I know it's your favorite."

"Yes! I love that place," Ryder yelled down over the loft railing.

At seven, Dominick and Ryder walked into the Cheesecake Factory. It was a Monday and not too crowded. In fact, there was only one very sexy lady waiting on a bench, probably for her date. He didn't get a good look at her face, because just as he was close enough, she stood and turned her back to them. Not that he minded, because her back side presented quite a distractingly, sexy view. With her cell phone pressed against her ear, he doubted she even noticed him.

"Right this way," the hostess said and led them to a booth on the back side of the restaurant.

Dominick and Ryder followed her, while he struggled to tear his eyes from the sexy lady. He wondered if she was waiting for a girl-friend or a guy. What was wrong with him? He usually didn't react this way, maybe it had to do with the whole internet dating thing. It had forced him to think about *seriously* dating again, for the first time in five years. Even after being seated, his eyes continued straining to see who her date was.

"Dad?" Ryder asked.

"Yes?" Dominick knew he appeared totally distracted, but kept his eyes on the door.

"What are you looking at?" Ryder appeared perplexed by his behavior.

"Nothing." He observed a man approach and shake the sexy lady's hand. Inadvertently, she turned towards his booth, for only a moment, before being led to a table near the window. He couldn't believe his eyes! She was beautiful and he could've sworn she looked exactly like the profile pictures of *LoveRocks*! He was totally losing it. This whole internet dating thing was getting to him. No way was it possible that they were the same woman.

"Dad, are you still staring at that lady who was waiting at the door? Yes, you are, aren't you?" Ryder asked. "I'm totally astonished to see you this interested in a woman."

"No. It's just that she looks so very familiar to me. It's almost uncanny the resemblance to—" Dominick stated, but stopped.

"I think you should seriously start dating again, Dad. It's been over five years. Mom wouldn't have wanted you to be alone for the rest of your life. She'd want you to find someone and to be happy."

Dominick's eyes teared up a bit at her declaration. "It's just that I don't know if I can love anyone else as much as I loved your mother. It wouldn't seem fair to them, if I couldn't do it."

"Well, you never know if you don't give it an honest try. Maybe you should try one of those internet dating sites. I heard they work well for people your age," Ryder offered.

At this suggestion, he almost choked on his drink of water. He set the glass down and stared at her. "You really think they can work?" Dominick asked, curious that she thought they might be legit and offer good matches for people his *age*.

"Sure. It seems like a good way to meet other people who are looking for someone to have a relationship with. I think you should give it a try."

"Maybe, I'll have to check them out." Dominick wondered if he should tell her about his research project. Ultimately, he decided it would be best if no one knew about it until he was finished and turned in the thesis which would eventually be his next book.

"I think she was a very pretty older lady," Ryder said.

"Well, thanks. It's good to know you approve of my taste in older women." He smirked.

Dominick and Ryder ordered dinner and cheese cakes for dessert. They had just received the check when the woman that looked like *LoveRocks* walked past their row of booths on her way to the restrooms.

She glanced his direction just as Dominick happened to look up and their eyes met for a moment, but she kept walking. When she exited the restroom, she didn't look his way. Instead, she proceeded to her table where she picked up her jacket, then was escorted out to the parking lot by her date.

Dominick wanted to run after her, but that had to be the most ridiculous idea he'd had in years. Instead, he paid the check and walked out to the parking lot to go home with his daughter. The entire drive home, he kept remembering the woman's face from the restaurant because this woman was beautiful and he definitely wanted to meet her.

Shortly after they arrived home, Ryder said, "I'm going out with Jenny and Sara for a few hours, so I'll be home later."

"Sure. Have fun and don't stay out too late," Dominick said.

"I know, Dad. If I decide to stay at their place, I'll call you." She picked up her coat, purse and keys, then left.

He walked into his office to check his emails. It appeared there were a couple more responses, but he didn't feel like dealing with them right away. He was tired and it'd been a long day. Absently, he reached over to pick up *LoveRocks'* file and flipped it open to her pictures. No way! It was her! That was why she looked so familiar. She'd looked even more beautiful in person.

Dominick hadn't wanted anyone in a long time.

But he wanted her.

# CHAPTER 9

*R*ocki pondered her situation on the dark winding road home from Edina. It wasn't that she felt displeased with the date, because she wasn't. *SunSetter* had proved to be very interesting and the conversation certainly hadn't been difficult at all. In fact, it had been extremely interesting. Sonny owned a Larson boat dealership in Minnetonka, thus the *SunSetter* name. According to him, there simply weren't any sunsets to compare to those seen on Lake Minnetonka. Rocki was a bit more prone towards the sunsets on Prior Lake being the best around the Twin Cities, but of course they were both biased. Just a little bit. He seemed like a nice guy and she regretted the fact that she hadn't felt any chemistry. The man was nice looking but no luck.

Oh well, this was what it was all about, playing the odds and going through the numbers until you met the one where the chemistry came alive in every fiber of your being. After all, this was only the first date. She hadn't really thought she would fall in love with the first guy she met. In fact, she didn't actually think she believed in love at first sight.

She was home, ready to change into something comfortable and relax in front of the TV. Minutes later, she sat on the couch in her Great Room searching the show listings on her streaming stations to find a Romantic Comedy to watch, finally settling on an old favorite, *Fools Gold*. Her curiosity was killing her, as she powered up her laptop, to check her emails.

Her cell phone rang with Allisa's ring tone. "Hello, Allisa."

"Rocki, how did it go? I've been dying to find out."

"Okay. He was nice but no chemistry on my part anyway. How was your date?" Rocki asked.

"Probably about the same. He was okay but really didn't do it for me," Allisa said. "We mustn't become down hearted. The search has only just begun and we may need to go through many men in order to find our soul mates," she added in her bad British accent.

"Soulmate is what you're looking for?" Rocki asked.

"Well, a girl can always dream. Right?" Allisa asked.

"Of course."

"You have a date every night too, don't you?" Allisa asked.

"You bet. I want to find my guy as soon as possible. Mainly, so I will have someone to have earth shattering sex with," Rocki stated with conviction.

"Well, that is a valid point to take into consideration. I have a date tomorrow too. So, who knows what will happen," Allisa said.

"You know something weird happened tonight though. I usually don't pay attention to men when I'm out, but at the Cheesecake Factory, I saw a guy about our age that came in while I was waiting for Sonny, who caught my attention. He was very nice looking and it had been very apparent that he was checking me out. I'm going to assume the young woman he was with was his daughter, but then it really doesn't matter since I'm sure I will never see him again."

"Well, it's good to know you've finally started noticing the men around you…. That at least, means you're still alive. I was beginning to wonder."

"Oh hush, you know damn well I'm still alive," Rocki retorted.

"Now, I'm going to get going since it's a work night. I do need my beauty sleep if I'm expected to function at the office tomorrow."

"I'm tired too. It's been a long day. I'll call you tomorrow." Rocki turned the phone off and quickly maneuvered her way to the Life Match site.

She wasn't sure why, but she was looking for a response from *Mr.Wrong*. And sure enough there it was. She quickly read:

*LoveRocks,*

*I am disappointed to hear you have a previous engagement, but we can reschedule. I'd love to meet you Saturday night at nine at Redstone's in Eden Prairie. Wear something sexy. I'm anxious to see if you look as good as your picture. This time I'm not taking no for an answer, so if you have plans cancel them. See you Saturday night.*

*Nick*

He couldn't possibly be serious! He was delusional that had to be it. Telling her to dress sexy? Totally crazy. No wonder he was on this site. He had to be looking for crazy women who would do whatever he ordered them to do. She hated to disappoint him, but that wasn't her style. But she was curious. She certainly wanted to see his face and that was something he hadn't responded to. Unfortunately, her curiosity was getting the best of her. What would one drink hurt? She was absolutely positive once she met him, she would be so done with him.

*Traveler* had responded and wanted to meet her on Friday night.

*HarleyGuy* responded for Sunday afternoon.

This would work out except she didn't have a date for Saturday night. She wasn't sure why she'd just referred to it as a date. It was a meeting. This was beginning to feel like an omen or something. Well, she could definitely spend Saturday night at home by herself.

Rocki hit reply on *Mr.Wrong's* email. She merely typed—

*Mr.Wrong,*

*No, thanks! Not Interested.*

*LoveRocks*

Then she typed emails to *Traveler* and *HarleyGuy* to confirm their meeting times and turned off her laptop.

Rocki got ready for bed because she desperately needed to get some good quality sleep. Her co-workers would be expecting the scoop on her dates. They would be proud she hadn't accepted dates from *Mr.Wrong*.

Her clothes were laid out for tomorrow, and she was ready for bed. Her reply would probably be the end of *Mr.Wrong*. Had she done the right thing? Oh well, if she changed her mind, she could always email him tomorrow.

# CHAPTER 10

*D*ominick's curiosity had gotten the better of him and he walked back into his office to check his emails one more time before he went to bed. There it was. *LoveRocks'* reply.

*Mr.Wrong,*

*No, thanks! Not interested.*

*LoveRocks*

He could see she was quite the challenge. Wasn't that what all bad boys wanted—challenge, conquest and then move on to the next challenge. He wondered if she realized this was exactly what she was doing—playing the game exactly right to get a bad boy. *Possibly not.* In fact, she must've just arrived home after a date which was why she had replied now. He was pretty sure it was her having dinner at the Cheesecake Factory. She must've not been interested in the guy since she was on the internet checking her emails already. Right? Oh Hell, he had no clue how this whole process was supposed to work and neither did most people, which is why he was doing this research project anyway. It wasn't anything personal, right? So why was he so interested in what *LoveRocks* was doing tonight? Well, if she thought that was the end of it, she was totally mistaken. He thought about it for a few minutes and then sent her a reply.

*LoveRocks,*

*Are you so afraid of bad boys that you can't even bring yourself to meet me face to face? I dare you. Redstone's Eden Prairie, Saturday night at nine.*

*Nick*

He felt better now. And he didn't want to deal with her reply till tomorrow, so he turned the computer off and went to bed.

～

THE NEXT MORNING, Dominick headed to the Starbucks in Prior Lake to meet *LadyInWaiting* for coffee at eight thirty before she went to work. LaVonne was a realtor and didn't have to be in the office until ten. She was divorced and had three children, with only the youngest, a senior in high school, still at home. Her ex had met someone else while she was busy trying to sell houses day and night, including weekends to support them.

She was not his type at all, so after chatting for 45 minutes...he left.

When he got back home, Ryder was still sleeping. He woke her up and went down to the kitchen to bake some cinnamon rolls for breakfast, before she was off to the Mall of America. Then he would be off for his lunch date.

"Daddy, I have been thinking about what we talked about last night and I think you really should check out the internet dating sites," Ryder stated, as she walked into the kitchen in her bathrobe.

"You do, huh?" Dominick slowly released a laugh he was holding back.

"Dad! I'm serious!"

"I know. I will take a look at some sites this afternoon and report back to you tonight. Okay?"

"Deal." Ryder smiled.

The timer went off for the rolls, so Dominick took them out of the oven and set out two plates on the table.

Ryder sat down and immediately served herself a roll.

He sat down too, helped himself to a roll and picked up the newspaper to read today's news.

She talked about how things were going at college and Dominick listened. When they were done, she went upstairs to shower and get ready for her *'Shop Till You Drop'* day at Mall of America.

Dominick knew it would be at least an hour before she came back down. He went to his computer and checked his emails to be sure everything was still on for today. It was time to send her—*LoveRocks*—another email, but from *Mr.Right* this time.

*LoveRocks,*

*I found your profile extremely interesting. I do think we would have a lot of things in common and could possibly be a good match. I tend to take things a bit slowly in the beginning as I like to get to know the other person first through email, before meeting.*

*My idea of a great first date would be to go to a good steak house for dinner, have some great California wine along with intellectually intoxicating conversation where we could become better acquainted.*

*What would your idea of a great date be?*

*Dom*

Dominick hit send. The goal was to make her fall in love with *Mr.Right*. He wasn't sure how long he could keep her hanging on without sending a picture. He actually liked the email, so he proceeded to send it to all the other women who he'd sent emails to as *Mr.Wrong* only this time from *Mr.Right*. It would actually be good for his research to see how many would keep emailing him without the picture being sent out. Although, he had to admit he was mainly concerned about how long *LoveRocks* lasted.

He just finished up his notes for the thesis when Ryder came down stairs finally dressed for her big shopping day.

Ryder came in and gave him a hug, then sat down on the chair next to him. She glanced at the computer to see what he was working on. "What are you working on today, Dad?"

"Notes on my project for my Master's Thesis. Are you ready to go?" he asked, trying to change the subject, as he wasn't ready to get into what his thesis was about with her.

She stood up from her chair.

Dominick knew she was waiting for him to offer further explanation. Now wasn't the time. He got out of his chair and walked her into the foyer. "Need some money for shopping?" He smiled at her.

"I'd love it, Dad," she said.

Dominick reached into his pocket for the money clip and handed her a hundred-dollar bill. "Have fun."

"Thanks, Dad," Ryder said and reached up to give him a hug as he was about six feet tall to her five foot two inches. She picked up her purse off the hall bench and reached in for her keys. "I won't be back till about nine. See you then."

"Have fun."

She went out the garage door to her car.

Dominick breathed a sigh of relief, thankful she hadn't pursued questioning him about his thesis at this time. He would tell her about it later. Hopefully, not until it was finished.

After he heard the garage door shut, he put on a jacket and went out the garage door to his car. Thankfully, he wouldn't be late for his lunch date at Panera in Shakopee with *ScarletLady*.

She was a redhead, thus the name and her name was Cari. They ordered lunch—sandwiches and soup duos—then found a table. Cari had a boutique store in the Burnsville Common's Shopping Landing called the Scarlet Lady. Surprise, surprise. She was divorced but had no children and wasn't interested in children at all. Thankfully, she had to get back to work, so an hour later he was on his way home.

He typed in a few notes about their meeting for his file. Even if he were looking, he would not go out with her again. Her dislike of children had completely turned him off. How did people get so greedy that it was only about them 24-7?

He clicked on his Life Match window and saw he had twenty-four replies to the *Mr.Right* emails he'd sent out earlier. Wow! Did none of these women work? Well, even if they did, they must have access to the internet and be free to use it while working. He would wait until tomorrow and send out another mass email reply.

He searched to see if there was one from *LoveRocks*. She hadn't replied to either one yet, so she probably was actually busy working. Hopefully, tonight he would get to read her replies. But then again, maybe she wouldn't get to them until later since she undoubtedly had a date tonight. He likewise had a date.

Enough of this email stuff and dating. Dominick went down to his workout room, changed, and started pumping weights. After which, he would ride the bike for an hour and then soak in the hot tub on the deck.

He needed to stop thinking about *LoveRocks*.

## CHAPTER 11

Rocki couldn't wait to get to work to tell her coworkers about her evening. Not that the date was fabulous, but it had been okay. Unfortunately, what she couldn't wait to tell them was about the gall of *Mr.Wrong* and his emails.

Tonia, her co-worker, had taken a switcheroo opinion. "I say go out with him. Sometimes, you just have to do it, so you can get them out of your system."

"Seriously, you don't actually mean to *do it*?" Rocki asked.

"Well, no I didn't, but come to think of it, you haven't had sex for a while, right?" Tonia asked, while stating a fact Rocki really didn't want broadcast.

"Shhhh. Not so loud." Rocki was embarrassed. "That's beside the point. And it doesn't mean I'm going to sleep with the first guy I meet."

"Well, they do have to ask you first if you know what I mean. And his body is hot, right?" Tonia asked. "Isn't this all part of why you're trying this? You did want to find someone to have hot sex with?"

"I guess so," Rocki replied somewhat sadly. "I do want to have sex with a hot guy, of course. Who wouldn't?"

"So, what's the problem? Why did you tell him no?" Tonia asked.

"Well, I want to fall in love again, too."

"Those are two different things. Although sometimes you can get lucky and find them both in one man."

Rocki was so confused. She had no idea what was the right decision to make in this situation. "He may not email me back after I told him no again."

"Bad boys like a challenge. He'll email you."

"Okay, if he emails me again, I'll meet him."

On her morning break, Rocki had a chance to check her emails. She read his response email.

*LoveRocks,*

*Are you so afraid of bad boys that you can't even bring yourself to meet me face to face? I dare you. Redstone's Eden Prairie, Saturday night at nine.*

*Nick*

She realized she'd been holding her breath as she read it. She felt so relieved to see his response of still wanting to meet her, she sighed heavily after reading it. There could only be one response to that email after the way her body had reacted. Even though it went against her better judgment, she would meet him. She was definitely going to get him out of her system one way or another. Hopefully, it wouldn't come to the other way. Oh Hell, what was she thinking? Having sex with him was probably a win-win situation. He would get what he wanted—at least she suspected that was his goal, what with asking her to wear something sexy—and she would get to have some hot sex to get her out of the way too long *no sex* streak with no strings attached. And of course, if the sex turned out totally bad, she wouldn't have to ever see him again.

Her break was over and she felt absolutely sure she was losing her mind totally to have spent the past fifteen minutes thinking about having hot sex with a man she hadn't even met!

"He emailed me. He still wants to meet on Saturday night." Rocki relayed to Tonia what the email said.

"There you go. I knew he would. This time, you better say yes," Tonia said.

"I think I will take him up on his offer to meet. I just want to get this over with," Rocki said.

On her lunch break, Rocki went back on the Life Match site to access her emails. This time, she sent *Mr.Wrong* a reply.

*Nick,*

*I accept your dare.*

*LoveRocks*

She quickly scrolled through her other emails and found one from *Mr.Right*. Her heart skipped a beat as she read his response.

*LoveRocks,*

*I found your profile extremely interesting. I do think we would have a lot of things in common and could possibly be a good match. I tend to take things a bit slowly in the beginning as I like to get to know the other person first through email, before meeting.*

*My idea of a great first date would be to go to a good steak house for dinner, have some great California wine along with intellectually intoxicating conversation where we could become better acquainted.*

*What would your idea of a great date be?*

*Dom*

Of course, it figured. He didn't ask her out, no he wanted to take it slow. She would email him back later. This may work out for the best though, because this way she could get Nick out of her mind before she met Dom.

Rocki spent the day thinking about having sex with Nick. Thank heavens it was finally time to go home and get ready for her date with *GuyForYou*.

On her way to meet *GuyForYou* at Perkins, she called Allisa. "Are you on your way to meet your date?" Rocki asked.

"Yup, how about you?" Allisa asked.

"Almost there. You'll never guess what I did today."

"What?"

"I accepted a date with *Mr.Wrong*, Nick, for Saturday night," Rocki stated.

"Wow! Really? I think you made the right decision. It's best to get it over with, so you don't have to wonder."

"Not so fast. I said a date not sex," Rocki clarified.

"I have a weird feeling that once you meet him, you'll want to go to bed with him. We'll simply have to wait and see, won't we?" Allisa teased.

"Right. We'll just see what happens on Saturday."

"I'm here."

"How about you, any hopes tonight's guy will be the one?" Rocki asked her.

"Not really but we'll see how it goes. How about your date for tonight?"

"I don't know, he picked Perkins. That may say it all right there. Talk to you later." Rocki ended the call and pulled into a parking spot.

*GuyForYou's* name was Guy. He was a car salesman. She had always had a severe distrust for car salesmen because they always told you lies. They would tell you anything they thought you wanted to hear, if they thought it meant they could sell you a car. Guy lived up to every expectation she had of him. Oh, and they were cheapskates also, always wanting everything for themselves. Thus, they had ended up at Perkins. Well, it wasn't breakfast time so she ordered a steak dinner. After all, he had said to order whatever she wanted. So, she did. She would never be seeing him again, so she totally didn't care. No, she was far more interested to get home and see if Nick had sent a gloating reply. As soon as they were done eating, she ended the date and went home.

Once she was home, she checked her emails. Nothing yet. It was still early and he probably had a date tonight, too. She would not think about his other dates. No, she needed to pay bills and workout on her bike. She would check the emails before bed and send *Mr.Right* her reply then.

At ten thirty, she had her laptop in hand and checked her emails from Life Match. Nothing new from Nick. He may be busy so she would have to wait. She needed to send *Mr. Right*, Dom, a reply to his email.

*Dom*

*Your description of a great date sounds perfect to me. I love steak. I love a good glass of wine. And I love intelligent conversations on interesting rele-vant topics.*

*I would love to hear about your child. Boy or girl? How old? I have two children, a boy and a girl who are both in college.*

*LoveRocks*

She hit send.

There were about ten new emails from new guys. She sorted through them and sent off short replies quickly, feeling like she was being repetitious, but what other choice was there if you wanted to keep up with all the emails?

Her clothes were set out for tomorrow and still no reply from Nick. Rocki turned off her laptop and called it a night.

# CHAPTER 12

*D*ominick finished his workout and got ready for his meeting with *GypsyWoman*. He was meeting her at The Cove in Prior Lake for dinner.

Her car pulled up right after he parked. *GypsyWoman*, Sasha, was definitely a free spirit. She wore a long flowing skirt with sheets of thin fabrics in layers and her top was only a couple of layers of flimsy fabric, secured by a belt adorned with an ornate brass cat in the center. Long black hair, lightly curled and in disarray, hung around her heart shaped face with dark brown eyes. In her strange way...she was a beautiful woman.

"Sasha?" Dominick asked.

"Yes. And you are Nick?" Sasha asked.

"I am, let's get a table," he said as he walked to the door and opened it for her.

Sasha proved to be an interesting woman. She was into fortune telling, which was quite the rage again, at least according her it was. She never married and had no children. Considering she missed out on a large part of life, children, she seemed to be a happy person who knew who she was. Unfortunately, she wasn't someone he would be interested in. No, definitely not what he was looking for...if he was looking.

The dinner was pleasant and when they were done, he paid the bill, wished her well, then drove home.

At home, he sat down at his desk in his office to check his Life Match emails, before Ryder got home. He quickly typed in his notes on his date with *GypsyWoman* and then opened his Life Match account.

He immediately saw the email from *LoveRocks*, Rocki. He'd actually been afraid he wouldn't hear from her again and really didn't want her to think she was being stalked or anything like that. He opened the email, assuming to read a scathing reply or another simple no.

*Nick,*

*I accept your dare.*

*LoveRocks*

"Yes!" he shouted.

He felt both excited and relieved. *LoveRocks* didn't know what he looked like but he knew what she looked like. Definitely the type of woman he liked. She looked damn sexy and downright stunning.

It had gotten late though and he would wait to send her a reply tomorrow. Hell, he didn't want to seem any more eager than he already had by pushing her too hard.

He scrolled down further and saw her email to *Mr.Right*. She had bought into his wanting to take it slow! Yes! He would send her a reply email tomorrow. He had to drag it out as long as he could, because after he met her on Saturday as Nick, he wouldn't be able to meet her as Dom. Hell, he hoped he wasn't blowing something good by playing this game with her. Maybe, he could explain things later, if he absolutely had to.

He sent off a few more reply emails and just turned off the computer when Ryder came home.

"Dad, I'm home." Ryder walked into his office.

Dominick got up and met her half way to give her a hug. "How was your day?"

"I had a blast with Jenny and Sara. We shopped all day and had dinner at Famous Dave's."

"I see you made purchases." He glanced toward her bags.

"Don't worry, Dad. Everything I bought on sale." Ryder laughed. "Just like Mom taught me."

"Good. I wasn't worried though."

"Do you have any ice cream? Do you want have some with me? And then I can show you what I bought." Ryder brought her bags into the Family Room and went to check out the freezer.

"I picked some up last week, so your favorite, Chocolate Chip, is in there," Dominick said He walked over to the counter where she put the container. "I'll scoop it."

Ryder pulled out her bargain finds from the MOA, holding them up for him to see.

She reminded him so much of her mother. He mainly watched to make sure they weren't too sexy for a young girl to be wearing. After all, he was a man and he knew firsthand what all those young college guys were thinking and looking at. "What time are you leaving for Gustavus?"

"I have a ten o'clock class, so about eight."

They talked for at least an hour about her friends at college, her classes, and any new boys she'd met.

After Ryder retreated to her bedroom, he walked into his master suite finally ready to call it a day. He pulled the sheets over him and laid there thinking about how nice it would be to have a woman in his bed again. His thoughts immediately drifted to *LoveRocks*. He couldn't stop thinking about this woman! Maybe after meeting her, he could stop thinking about her. But he had the strange feeling that it would be exactly the opposite.

# CHAPTER 13

*M*orning arrived with the sun streaming brightly through the crack in the blinds where he hadn't pulled them all the way closed. Dominick got out of bed and put on a robe. It was seven and he wanted to be up to see Ryder before she left. He walked out of his room and heard the water running in her shower. Good, she was up. The smell of coffee wafted up the staircase. Thank heavens for coffee makers with start timers, because the aroma was heavenly. He walked back to his master suite to take a shower before having his coffee.

Sitting at the breakfast counter in the kitchen with his mug, he waited for Ryder.

"Dad? You down here?" Ryder asked as she walked into the kitchen.

"Yes, just waiting for you," he said.

"Thanks, Dad," she said.

"You all packed? Want any breakfast?"

"No, got to go, so I'm not late for class."

Dominick got up and walked her to the garage. He embraced Ryder and kissed her cheek. "Love you, Baby. Drive safe."

He closed her car door after she got in her shiny new red Mustang convertible, watched her back out of the garage and leave.

He closed the garage door and went back into the very large and empty house. It hadn't felt so empty before, but now he was noticing the emptiness and realized he finally wanted to move past his loneliness after Anna's death and start living again. Maybe this thesis was trying to tell him something with the whole dating thing.

Time to email *LoveRocks*. Dominick filled his thermal cup with the hazelnut mocha coffee he had brewed earlier and made his way into the office. Her file, *LoveRocks*, was on the top of the potential Life Match possibilities. He'd lost all interest in the others. First, the response to her email to *Mr.Right*.

*LoveRocks,*

*So good to hear back from you! We will have to try out the great date scenario on our first date. Later, once we get to know each other better.*

*I have one daughter, who is a very special part of my life. We are very close and have a great relationship. She attends Gustavus College in St. Peter and comes home whenever she can.*

*What do you like to do on a cold snowy Saturday night?*

*Dom*

He thought it sounded pretty good if he didn't say so himself. He hit send.

He glanced at the clock and saw it was already eight thirty and he had a coffee date at nine. It was time to go meet *HarleyGirl*.

Dominick pulled into the Caribou Coffee shop at five to nine. He walked in to see Hailey, the Harley girl, seated at a table next to the window, wearing a Harley Davidson black V-neck long sleeved shirt with the Harley Davidson logo in gold. She had large breasts, revealing ample cleavage for all to see. Her long, white-blonde, straight hair hung over her breasts leaving tiny spaces to the imagination.

This woman was indeed striking but was a bit over the top for him.

"Hailey?" he said as he walked up to her table.

She extended her hand. "Yes, and you must be Nick."

Dominick had also worn his Harley black t-shirt, jeans and Harley boots. He even threw on his black leather jacket to play the part of the bad boy to the tee. He was decked out yes, but he hadn't ridden his Harley Davidson Soft Tail today.

"What would you like to drink?" Dominick asked.

"A Mocha Frappuccino. Thanks," Hailey answered.

Dominick put his jacket on the chair across from her and walked over to the counter to order their drinks. He also ordered a piece of pumpkin spice bread and a piece of marble pound cake.

The conversation leaned toward the whole biker world, which he knew all too well, as he had attended various biker events in town and even made it out to Sturgis with some of his biker friends, a couple of times recently in the past five years.

Hailey proved to be very interesting and even had her own Fat Boy Harley Davidson. By day, she was a beautician which enabled her to pick her own schedule to fit her biking needs.

An hour later, he was on his way home. Once there, he was at his desk typing in his notes about his date with Hailey, *HarleyGirl*. He actually only had favorable things to say about her. She was hot, but his mind was focused on *LoveRocks*.

Now to type a reply to her response to *Mr.Wrong's* email. He had been thinking of what to write back ever since he'd received her reply. It needed to be short and to the point.

*LoveRocks,*

*Glad to see you like dares.*

*They are what you want them to be.*

*Let's make it dinner on Saturday at seven at Redstone's.*

*Nick*

Yes, he liked it. Sounded pretty damned good. Dominick hit send. He couldn't wait to see what her reply was, because he was looking forward to having dinner with her.

He checked his other emails and sent out a few responses. He didn't have a lot of time, since he had a lunch date with *SuzyQ* and her name just happened to be Suzy. Yeah, what a coincidence. He was meeting her at noon at Panera Bread in Shakopee, so he needed to get going.

He quickly changed his shirt, as he only wore it earlier for Hailey's sake, and put on a white button-down shirt instead. He took the Escalade and pulled into the Panera parking lot at ten to twelve to wait for Suzy.

She pulled in promptly at noon. She had short black hair and a great little petite body.

He got out of the car to meet her.

She turned when she saw him approach the door, "Nick?"

"Yes, and you are Suzy?" He held the door open for her.

They went in, ordered lunch, then sat at a table near the fireplace and made small talk.

Suzy was a seamstress and worked on costumes at the St. Olaf University in Northfield. She was a very pleasant, divorced lady with two children in high school. Very down to earth. Very likeable.

An hour and a half later, they said their goodbyes.

Dominick stopped at the grocery store on his way home to pick up a few things. Once at home, it was time for more notes, this time on Suzy, *SuzyQ*.

He spent the afternoon, working on emails and setting up meetings for the next week, only he cut it down to three a day instead of four. This was actually beginning to feel like a full-time job. Maybe he would be enjoying it more next week. He could only hope that after he met *LoveRocks*, he would be able to get her out of his mind.

He was meeting *LadyInRed*, Lainey, at five thirty at Dangerfield's in Shakopee. He arrived at five fifteen and walked into the lobby to see a gorgeous lady with wavy red hair about shoulder length.

"So, what brought you to Life Match?" Dominick asked, trying to get more fodder for his future book.

"I was tired of going to the bars to look for men when I don't drink hardly at all," Lainey said.

They ordered dinner and talked about dating at their age, and how it had changed from when they were young.

At seven thirty, she hugged him and said good bye. It was a good thing he had set all his meetings close to home, because otherwise, he wouldn't be able to go home in between.

Once home, he typed in his notes on Lainey. He then looked for an email from *LoveRocks*. Nothing yet. Then left to meet *SexyLady* at the Legends Club, in Prior Lake for drinks at nine. Slade was a legal assistant. Her body was full of curves and any man would love to wake up next to her. But he still was hoping he could wake up next to *LoveRocks*.

# CHAPTER 14

The next day at work, Rocki shared her not so great date with Guy, *GuyForYou*. The girls got a chuckle out of her ordering the steak at Perkins. After all, who orders steak at Perkins anyway? Someone who had the misfortune of having dinner with a used car salesman, and one she had never met before to top it off.

She told them about accepting Nick's dare and they were ecstatic!

"You'll see. He'll end up being the one you fall for, mark my words," Penny said.

"I doubt it. I'm simply going out with him to prove to myself that I am not interested in him," Rocki stated.

"We'll see," Judy said.

"It's going to be a long wait till Saturday night," Penny said.

"You guys are crazy! It's only an hour of conversation, which will be all about how much I dislike bad boys!" Rocki said, dumbfounded they thought she would actually like this guy.

"So, who's the lucky guy tonight?" Judy asked.

"*JazzMan.*"

"Well, that may be fun. Is he a musician?" Penny asked.

"His name is Jason and he plays in a jazz band on the weekends for a hobby," Rocki informed them. She did think he sounded interesting and she was looking forward to meeting him at Bonfire tonight.

It was time to get back to actually working now. So, the conversation ended abruptly when their boss walked through the office.

During her lunch break, she checked her emails and saw one from *Mr.Wrong* telling her they would be having dinner instead of only a drink at Redstone's. She wasn't sure how she felt about having dinner. It would be a longer time she would need to spend with him and what if it didn't go well? It could then end up being a very long evening. But then again, if she had to spend the evening with him making the moves on her, she might as well at least get to eat dinner. And he would definitely be buying since he'd asked her to dinner.

She sent *Mr.Wrong* a reply.

*Nick,*

*Invitation to dinner accepted.*

*Rocki*

Yes, it was brief and to the point, which was definitely the message she wanted to send him, so she hit send.

After work, she went home to change clothes for her date with the *JazzMan*. She'd been looking forward to meeting Jason.

On her drive to Bonfire, she listened to a commercial on the radio advertising Life Match and the high percentage of marriages among their customers. She laughed because she found it hard to believe this whole process worked that well. Since she'd just started, she didn't feel she could accurately forecast her odds of finding Mr. Right on the site. But as strange as it may seem as a way to meet the love of your life, she did think it warranted giving it a chance. So here she was. . .meeting Jason, the *JazzMan*.

Rocki walked in and saw a man look her way immediately, then walk towards her.

"Rocki, I presume." Jason watched for her response.

"Yes," she answered.

"I'm Jason." He motioned her towards a high table by the bar.

She walked over to it and sat down.

Jason was about 5'10" with medium length light brown hair and a neatly trimmed beard. His smile was incredible and made him all the more handsome.

The waitress took their drink order which was wine and Jason took the liberty of ordering a couple of appetizers for them.

"So, Rocki, what do you do?" he asked.

"I work at the local Prior Lake Newspaper in the office. What I really like is photography and every once in a while, I manage to sell a few to the newspaper. I guess you'd say photography is my passion. It sounds like music is yours."

"Yes, I've been playing guitar and singing since I was young. It simply wasn't enough to pay the bills though, so I had to get a real job. I have a custom framing shop. On the weekends, I get to do what I love and make music.

They talked about their lives, their likes and dislikes and they laughed while they munched on the appetizers and slowly savored their glasses of wine.

"Can I call you?" Jason asked.

Rocki liked him, so she gave him her photography business card for Sandstrom Photos.

Jason accepted the card and reached into his wallet to give her his card. He paid the bill and escorted her to her car.

Rocki anticipated his quick light kiss and felt a slight spark. She got in her car and he promised to call her, then left to walk to his SUV.

On the drive home, her smile was genuine and she looked forward to going out with Jason again.

Rocki had at least twenty new emails on Life Match, when she checked the site. Most, she was not interested in and deleted them, not that she was trying to be rude, it was just that she truly didn't have the time to respond to all of them every day. She tried to pick a couple each day to pursue further, so hopefully she would have five dates for next week.

*007* sounded interesting and she liked his screen name, so she responded to him for Tuesday night. Earlier, she had responded to

*RaceFan* for Monday night and he'd accepted. Keeping track of all these emails and keeping a calendar updated with new dates was like a second job. Hopefully, the payback would outweigh all the time spent in the pursuit of Mr. Right. She was completely convinced though, that *Mr.Wrong*, aka Nick, was not her Mr. Right!

# CHAPTER 15

*ominick smiled as he read Rocki's short and to the point email accepting his dinner invitation. Damn, but he was totally looking forward to meeting her. But it was only Thursday and today he had four new women to meet.

He showered after working out, dressed and was ready to meet Regan, *LakerGal*. They were to meet at the local downtown bakery Edelweiss for coffee, where he would be having one of their delicious chocolate croissants. Of course, she could have one too, or her choice from their mouthwatering pastries in the full glass display case.

After parking, he walked in the bakery to find a gorgeous blonde with shoulder length layered hair seated in a chair at a table by the fireplace. He walked over.

"Regan?" he asked looking into her baby blue eyes.

"Yes, and you must be Nick," she stated giving him the quick once over and smiled.

"I am," he said. "Let's get some coffee and rolls."

Regan stood and followed him up to the counter. They ordered coffees and two chocolate croissants then went back to the table.

"Nick, so why are you Mr. Wrong?" she bluntly asked.

"I've always been a ladies' man. I play hard, live hard, and have

66

never found commitment to one woman to be important to me. But on the other hand, I work hard, make good money, and know how to treat a woman to get what I want and need. And if she doesn't already know what she wants or needs, I can help give her what she needs." Dominick watched for her reaction.

She smiled.

"So do you know what exactly you want and what you need?" he asked.

"I do," she answered.

"And are they both the same?" he coaxed.

"I think they are," she said.

"Well, maybe you've met your match, *LakerGal*."

They chatted about her work as a real estate agent and he was intrigued with her mind as well as her body. Only problem was she had a five-year-old and he really didn't know if he wanted to raise another child. That would be another fifteen years of child rearing. Not that he didn't like children, he would just prefer a woman with grown children or at least high school age.

Before they left, she handed him her card. "Call me. Call anytime. I look forward to seeing you again." She got into her Tahoe and left.

Dominick was left standing at the curb. Wow! She was pretty damn sure of herself, of that he was certain. He needed to go out on a few second dates. So, what the Hell, she might as well be one of them. He'd call her, but he'd make her wait a few days at least.

A couple hours later, he pulled in to TG Fridays at the Burnsville Center after doing some shopping to pick up a couple extra bad boy shirts and jeans.

The female sales clerk assured him they were the latest trend and he would have all the women stopping to take a second look.

His lunch date was with Kim, *SkiBum*. She was a Yoga instructor. Yoga wasn't his thing, he'd tried it once a few years back and made that decision. Kim was tall, 5'9, slim and had brown hair spiked with blonde tips. She was nice looking, but definitely not his type. There was absolutely no chemistry going on there at all. They each ordered salads topped with a sliced chicken breast on top. The only thing they had in common basically was skiing, so that was what the conversation centered around during the entire meal. They talked about all the places they'd skied.

An hour later, they left and not a word was said about seeing each other again.

Dominick headed home. It had already been a long day. He hadn't done anything but have conversations with two women, but it had been draining just the same. If only Anna were still here, life would be so much simpler. But she wasn't and that fact would never change. Ever.

He needed to get some work done on his thesis, so he sat down at his desk and typed in notes on his two meetings. He scrolled through his emails on Life Match and sent out a couple replies. He looked through his matches and sent out a few new emails, too. He picked up *LoveRocks'* file and looked at her pictures. He wasn't sure why exactly but he was drawn to her. She definitely was beautiful, but it was more than that. He had the feeling she was a beautiful person on the inside, too, and he had every intention of finding out if he was right.

At five, he drove over to Apple Bees at the Burnsville Center to meet Valerie, *TravelBug*. Surprise, surprise. She was a travel agent. Valerie had wavy shoulder length hair and green eyes. She was petite about 5'1" and had a nice shape. He knew her the minute he walked in because she looked exactly like the pictures on her profile.

"Valerie, you look just like your picture. It's a pleasure to meet you," Dominick said.

She smiled. "You are a pleasant surprise. You never know what to expect when people don't post their pictures."

They sat at a high-top table and ordered drinks. Dominick was well traveled as was she, so the conversation was extremely interesting. They talked about places they'd been, places they'd heard about and of course, the places they still wanted to see.

Valerie gave him her business card, to call her for either business or pleasure. She laughed with her bubbly personality coming through vibrantly.

Dominick took the card and said, "I'm sure we'll talk again."

After she'd left, Dominick walked out to his Escalade. It was approaching seven and his next date was at seven thirty, so he had some time to kill in between. He drove over to Best Buy to take a look at the new televisions—not that he needed one, but it was always fun to see what was new.

At seven fifty, he pulled into the Outback Steakhouse parking lot. He walked in to find Maddie, *LadyMadonna*, seated on a bench waiting patiently.

"Hi, I'm Nick. You must be Maddie." Dominick reached out to shake her hand.

"I am. Glad to meet you," Maddie said.

He turned toward the hostess stand. "Table for two, please."

Dominick and Maddie followed the hostess to a booth. They opened the menus while the waitress took their drink order.

"Order whatever you want, my treat." He smiled at Maddie. "I'm having the New York Strip. What sounds good to you?"

"I think I'll have the Filet Mignon."

They waitress returned with their drinks then took their order.

"So, Maddie, what do you do?" Dominick asked.

"I have an art gallery on 50th and France in Edina."

"How very interesting. And how did you get into the business?"

Maddie shared her story about falling in love with art as a child and her journey to learn everything she could about art in high school and college.

Dominick tried to share as little as he could about what he did since it was a lie. He basically said he was in investments, which was partially the truth since he had quite a large amount of money in investments. Over the years, he had done his homework on investing and actually knew quite a lot about the field which made it easy to talk about the profession.

The conversation was interesting and the food mouthwateringly top-notch fare which made two hours fly by. Dominick found Maddie interesting but not for him. He could tell she was a great person and would make a great friend, but he knew he had to pass. He didn't want to lead her on when he knew it wouldn't go anywhere on his part.

Maddie gave Dominick her card. "Feel free to call. If not, feel free to stop in if you are in need of any unusual, one-of-a-kind art pieces."

"Thanks, I will keep your number. I'm sure I will be looking for some art pieces soon," Dominick said choosing his words carefully, so as not to lead her on unintentionally.

Maddie walked out the door with Dominick and turned to him once they were outside. "It was a pleasure to meet you." She then turned away and walked to her car.

Dominick was left standing there, knowing she was hurt, but in his book, it was better not to lead her on. He had a feeling though that he would be making an art purchase after the project was finished and the book was out.

Dominick walked to his Escalade and drove home. He felt guilty but knew he'd done the right thing and treated her fairly. It was the whole dating scene that bothered him, no matter if you did it the old-fashioned way or the new high-tech way. The high-tech way had its downfalls and profile pictures were a big one.

When he first walked into Outback, he would've guessed the woman on the bench was Maddie, just from her pictures. People always complained the people on dating sites didn't look like their pictures or they posted totally different people's pictures on their profiles. So far, everyone he'd met looked like their pictures. He couldn't imagine why anyone would think it would possibly do them any good to post someone else's picture, since once they met a potential match in person, it would be apparent they'd lied. Lying was not the way to start out any relationship. It was a good thing he wasn't looking for a match, since he was totally lying about everything. *Well, almost everything.*

# CHAPTER 16

*T*hank God it was Friday. The week was long when she really would rather be out taking photos of things that interested her. Friday was Rocki's half day at work so she was having a late light lunch with Allisa at Salads Plus. Later, they both had dinner dates. *HarleyGuy*, Harvey had finally got back to her and wanted to meet her at Whisky Junction for burgers.

Finally, it was two and she was on her way to meet Allisa at Panera.

"Rocki, glad you could fit me into your busy schedule!" Allisa said laughing, as she walked up to the door about the same time as Rocki.

"Me? You're the one that's too busy. Find a keeper yet?" Rocki asked as they approached the counter to order their salads.

"No. How about you?" Allisa answered.

They ordered and walked over to the next counter to pick up their food.

"Jason, the guy I met last night was interesting. I might go out with him on a second date." Rocki set her tray on the table and sat down. "But I'm not head over heels in love or anything like that."

"So why do you want to go out with him again then?" Allisa asked.

"We have common interests and the evening went well. Wouldn't mind kissing him." Rocki was beginning to second guess her decision to go on a second date. She did want to feel that overwhelming chemistry with someone again, like she had with her ex, Mark. But she wasn't totally sure she believed in 'Love at first sight.'

"Rocki? What's going through your mind?"

"Maybe, I shouldn't go out again with him. I don't think it will work out in the long run," Rocki said as reality set in.

"You have to remember no one is perfect, Rocki. No one will be a perfect match. There will be some differences," Allisa stated.

"I know. I just think I should be more excited about the aspect of going out with him again. And I'm not."

"How about the guy tonight? *HarleyGuy?*" Allisa asked.

"He's probably a total bad boy, too. Just like *Mr.Wrong*. Oh, my God! Why am I drawn to them?" Rocki asked.

"They do have a certain allure about them. It's probably the danger. The adventure. Wanting what you shouldn't have. We all are drawn to them. Might be a *fun* little relationship to experience, simply for the *Hell* of it. At this point in your life, you're entitled."

"I know, I married the good guy and look where that got me. Well, I can't complain totally. I did get Ashley and Trevor out of it. But, I also got a whole lot of heartache."

"It's okay to go out with them, just don't let your heart get involved and you'll be fine," Allisa said. "Don't forget you have *Mr.Wrong* tomorrow night."

"How can I forget?" Rocki said.

"I think if you're going to date a bad boy, it should probably be him. As long as he looks hot. He has all the toys and can probably show you a good time. Might be entertaining at least."

"You know what I think? I think you're losing it."

"Ah come on, I bet you've fantasized about a bad boy making hot crazy love to you the whole night long," Allisa teased.

"Yeah, right. It's a recurring dream of mine." Rocki laughed.

"How about you date a bad boy, if I do too?" Allisa proposed.

"How many dates do we have to go on to qualify as dating?" Rocki asked.

"I don't know. . .how about we see who can last the longest. Come on, it'll be fun. In fact, we'll probably have the time of our lives!" Allisa said.

"Okay, what the heck. Can't commit to it being *Mr.Wrong* though, till I see what he looks like. Gotta have the chemistry you know."

"Deal. I need to find a bad boy first. The guy I'm going out with tonight has a Harley, too. *BikerGuy*, Kirk. We'll see."

"Who do you have for Saturday night?" Rocki asked.

"*Stud*, Sam." Allisa laughed. "I should be able to pick one out of these two."

Rocki laughed.

"Hope it's *Mr.Wrong*, Nick, that you pick. He has a way of making your blood boil about his bad boy stuff, so if he can make you run hot for him—look out. Sparks will be flying for sure!" Allisa said.

They finished their salads and headed home to get ready for their dates. She needed to send a reply to *Mr.Right*, so she turned on her laptop to send him a quick response.

*Dom,*

*My daughter, Ashley, attends St. Olaf in Northfield and my son, Trevor, attends the University of Minnesota in Duluth. Both live on campus. We are close and they call almost every day and come home for breaks and holidays.*

*On a cold snowy Saturday night? Stay home. Cook dinner. Have a cup of hot chocolate by the fire. And read a good book, if I'm alone. Now, if I'm with a special someone, some snuggling would be in order. And you just never know what might happen. . .*

*Rocki*

Rocki stood in front of her closet trying to figure out what she should wear to a biker bar. She finally settled on a tight pair of jeans and a low-cut black top. A pair of heeled black leather boots and her black leather jacket should do the trick. After touching up her makeup and hair, she was on her way to the other side of town to Whiskey Junction. He'd mentioned a Blues band would be playing, so she hoped to do some dancing tonight.

Forty-five minutes later, Rocki pulled into the Whiskey Junction parking lot. She was lucky and found the last parking spot available.

Thankfully, the weather was nice, unseasonably warm. It had actually reached sixty-five today. It was cooling down quickly, though.

Rocki looked around at all the bikes. And all the biker guys. She was totally having second thoughts as to the safety of the situation. What had she been thinking to drive down here by herself and meet a strange man, she'd never met before? She must be losing her mind, was the only sane answer. She was actually starting to feel afraid for her well-being, which was why she was still sitting in her car.

She jerked slightly when she heard a knock on her window. She looked out to see Harvey. Yes, she knew it was him by the pictures he'd posted. She pushed the button to open the window.

"Rocki?" Harvey asked.

"Yes."

"I'm Harvey."

She felt a bit calmer now. He looked like his picture and seemed okay. "Let me close the window and grab my purse." Rocki closed the window, took a deep breath, opened the door and got out of the car, purse in hand.

Harvey backed up to let her out. Once she was out, he said, "Nice to meet you." He smiled at her with brilliantly white, straight teeth.

"Nice to meet you," Rocki said.

"Ready to go in? They have great burgers here. You do like burgers?" Harvey asked.

"Oh, yes," Rocki said and followed him inside Whiskey Junction. She noticed he was wearing nice jeans, boots, and a Harley leather jacket. He had brown hair, in a short cut, not shaved but not long either. He was actually quite good looking.

She followed him to a table and sat down.

He ordered burgers for them with fries and Miller draft beers.

They talked and ate their burgers.

Rocki felt more at ease.

"I have my own computer software company," Harvey said.

"Does that make you a computer geek?" Rocki asked laughing.

"I guess so. Is there such a thing as a Harley Geek?" Harvey laughed along with her.

"Not sure." Rocki shifted in her chair. The music was starting and soon, they would not be able to talk over it.

They listened to the music and danced the night away to the Blues. Harvey proved to be an excellent dancer and she enjoyed dancing with him. About midnight, she told him she needed to call it a night and they walked out to the parking lot.

"Let me show you my bike before you head out," Harvey said walking over to where only bikes were parked.

Rocki followed him to see rows and rows of parked bikes. Sadly, not knowing much about bikes, they all looked the same to her.

He proudly stopped in front of a black Harley with white paint designs and a back seat with a bar behind it.

Ok, so it was a motorcycle, was about all she could say about it. Weren't they all basically the same? Only different colors? Some had the back seat for a rider with a back rest and some didn't. Some had a windshield and some didn't. That about took care of it all.

"Nice bike," Rocki said. *Wasn't that what you were supposed to say?*

"Do you ride?" Harvey asked.

"Once."

"Care to go riding sometime?" he asked.

"I don't have the proper clothes for it," she answered.

"We can take care of that at a Harley store," Harvey said. "Here's my card. Call me if you're interested. I'm interested, so it's your call."

Rocki took the card, slid it inside her purse, and pulled her keys out as they walked over to her car.

She turned towards Harvey to say goodbye when they reached the car. There was chemistry. She knew that after slow dancing with him. He swiftly pulled her body to his and kissed her deep and long. She didn't have time to pull away because by the time she actually thought about it, the kiss was over and his arms were no longer around her.

He smiled at her and his eyes sparkled with mischief. "Definitely interested. Call me." He turned and walked away.

Rocki opened her car door, stepped in, and started the engine. "I guess so," she said.

He was interested. So was she. What was going on with her? She'd felt the strong attraction between them, too. Maybe it was just the dancing with her body up against his? Maybe, she'd gone too long without actually being with a man that her hormones had gone all wacky. He was all wrong for her. She was sure of that. Or was she? It was probably simply the whole bad boy thing. Hell, she didn't even know if she wanted to go riding on motorcycles at all. *Weren't they dangerous?*

Yeah, probably just as dangerous as the guys driving them.

# CHAPTER 17

*D*ominick woke the next morning eager to get the day started. Mainly, so he could move on to Saturday and his meeting with Rocki. First off, he would send her an email from *Mr.Right*. He poured himself a glass of orange juice since he would be drinking coffee at nine with *MarathonRunner*.

Seated at his desk, he signed into Life Match and scrolled to Rocki's reply to his *Mr.Right's* email. He had responded to others from his *Mr.Right* profile, but for those he used a canned response email he'd put together. For Rocki, his response would be genuine, so he wrote it from the heart.

*Rocki,*

*For a cold snowy Saturday night, I would grill steaks for dinner and have a glass of wine by the fire.*

*Oh, and I can't forget to mention we would be lying on the white fur rug in front of the fireplace hopefully shedding our clothes slowly piece by piece and making love.*

*How do you feel about riding Harleys?*

*Dom*

He hoped it wasn't too much for her at this point. He hit send.

At nine, he walked into Caribou Coffee in Lakeville and saw *MarathonRunner*, Tonia, walk in after him.

"Nick?" Tonia asked after seeing him at the counter.

"Yes. What would you like to drink?" he asked.

They both ordered coffees and muffins, then found a table to sit at.

"Out running already this morning?" Dominick asked noticing she was wearing a jogging outfit. He also noticed she was a bit heavier than the pictures she had on her profile.

"Yes, I try to run every morning. Didn't get out much last winter though and I'm afraid it shows," she said.

"Working out in the winter can be difficult. I like to ride a stationary bike in the winter," Dominick said.

"Wish I had one at home. It would be a lot easier than driving to the club."

Dominick kept the conversation light and short. Soon, they were both off to get on with their days. He definitely wasn't interested in Tonia. Not to be petty, but he wanted his woman to be in shape. He prided himself in taking care of his body by working out and trying to eat right and expected the same from any woman, he dated. It actually was Anna who had got him started on the whole exercise routine and after she died, he'd kept at it because it had become a part of his everyday routine by then. He missed working out with her.

Unfortunately, he didn't feel like Tonia could be anything but a friend but he admired her for trying to get into shape.

He headed home. There were more emails to answer on Life Match, then more matches to look at and initiate contact with. He even had one from Professor Drewberry, who was overseeing his thesis project, wondering how the whole dating thing was going. He hadn't checked in with Drewberry yet, so he sent him a detailed summary of his week. Drewberry would find it humorous, since he too, was single again and looking to meet a new woman.

Around eleven thirty, he headed to Olive Garden in Burnsville to meet *DancingQueen*, Nancy. She'd gotten there early and was waiting in the lobby when he arrived. They got a table and ordered pasta dishes.

"Dancing must be a part of your life," Dominick said.

"I have a dance studio in Burnsville." Nancy nodded.

"What kind of dance do you teach?" he asked.

"We teach tap, jazz, ballet, and hip hop for all ages. The only thing we don't teach is ballroom dancing."

"That must be rewarding. Teaching children, especially," Dominick said.

Nancy had a somewhat athletic build probably due to all the dancing. She was about 5'6" with long black hair and a round pretty face. She was a little too reserved for him though, so he talked about theater shows he'd seen where dance was the main theme. This got her talking more and they made it through lunch. He paid the check and they were both on their way again.

Wow, this was getting tougher. Maybe he had lucked out looks wise on the first ones, but they were at least more talkative. And interesting, too.

Once home, he typed in notes on his date. He worked on organizing his files on internet dating. He wasn't sure exactly how he would write his thesis. So right now, he was only gathering information. Once he was finished with the research, he certainly hoped he would figure out what the story would be about for his thesis.

Later, he dressed for an early dinner with *RomanticOne*, Mandy, at Fong's in Prior Lake for a Chinese dinner. Mandy was a tall woman about 5'10", reddish brown hair, shoulder length and layered to frame her face. Brown eyes and full pouty lips.

The hostess showed them to a table. Dominick sat down across from breasts on full view in her low-cut shirt. She definitely dressed to entice. And enticed he was. Mandy worked at Macy's selling make up. She was a make-up artist.

"So, tell me about yourself," Dominick finally managed to get out after the waitress took their order.

"I create beautiful people," Mandy said smiling, with total confidence of exactly what she did.

"They must be greatly appreciative," Dominick said, watching her beautiful face as she listened to him.

"Oh, they all love me," Mandy said.

"What do you do for fun?" Dominick asked, as his eyes feasted on her breasts.

"I go tanning. I like to keep this nice tan all year long. I go dancing at the clubs to keep in shape. It's great exercise, don't you think?" Mandy asked.

"You are obviously in great shape. And very tan," Dominick stated, as it was clearly visible for all to see.

"Oh and I go shopping. It's great exercise walking around the Mall of America."

Dominick was grateful that at that moment their dinner was served. Mandy was most definitely an air head. Most definitely hot. Most definitely air head.

When he was done feasting his eyes for the night, he paid the check and they walked to her car. He couldn't help himself, so he kissed her. Damn if he wasn't turning into, he wasn't sure what, but he had to wonder if his manhood was at stake here.

"Here's my number. Call me anytime," Mandy said and got in her car.

Dominick stood dumbfounded on the sidewalk and watched her drive out of the parking lot. What was wrong with him? He could've probably had some really great sex. Only a one-night stand. But no, she had just driven off. He knew he'd done the right thing. Hell, he would never be able to have a normal conversation with her much less an intelligent one. Yes, he had done the right thing. He slowly walked to his car.

Minutes later, he was home. He had a little time before his next date, so he decided to send Rocki another email before their meeting tomorrow.

*Rocki,*

*I am looking forward to seeing you face to face.*

*Tomorrow, you meet your match.*

*Nick*

He hit send.

Minutes later, he was on his way to meet *RoseLady*, Sela, at Buffalo

Wild Wings for a drink. After parking, he walked in, looked around, and didn't see anyone who resembled Sela's picture, so he sat down on a bench in the waiting area.

A few minutes later, a woman walked up to him. "Are you Nick?" she asked.

"Yes," Dominick answered.

"I'm Sela," she informed him.

Dominick was in shock. This woman was at least ten years older than her profile said, her hair was grey instead of blonde, and she weighed at least seventy-five pounds more than the woman in the pictures. He actually wanted to run right out the door. But he was a mature adult and he was doing this for his research, not for dates, so he had no reason to leave. In fact, this would be excellent research for his thesis. *Why would anyone do this?* He didn't have a clue, but he intended to find out.

"There's a table open over there, let's have a seat," Dominick said, as he watched for the reaction on her face. He saw shock. But she followed him to the table.

They sat down and ordered drinks from the waitress.

"So, tell me about yourself," Dominick said.

"I'm a florist, thus the profile name of *RoseLady*."

"So, whose picture did you post on your profile?" Dominick asked.

"My daughter's," Sela answered.

"Why didn't you post your picture?" Dominick asked.

"If I posted my picture, would you have met me?" Sela asked.

"To be honest, no. But by not posting your picture, you've lied to any potential matches you might receive. Were you honest about anything?" Dominick probed.

"Not really."

"How old are you, Sela?" Dominick asked.

"Old."

"What were you hoping to accomplish by doing this?" he asked.

Sela began crying. "You are the first person I've met."

"Do you think we would be a good match?" he asked.

"Probably not," she answered.

"If you change your profile picture, and write a bio about who you actually are, what you are honestly looking for and your correct age, you may be surprised," Dominick suggested.

"No one will contact me."

"I'm sure there are men your age, who don't have movie star faces but are good guys, looking for good women who don't have to look like a model. They are lonely and looking for companionship and love like you," he said.

"Thank you for being so kind. I will try it. Who knows maybe there is an ornery old man out there, looking for someone like me, who can put up with him. And maybe with some honey, he can change into just a plain old man," Sela said laughing.

Dominick smiled. He'd made her laugh and it felt good. He motioned for the waitress to bring their check. He paid the tab and walked out with Sela.

"Be sure and let me know if you find your Mr. Right." He walked to his car and left.

Well, if that didn't just about beat it all. He would've never thought lying on your profile like she had was actually happening out in the dating world. But it had. Actually, he was glad it had happened to him, because now he could write about it, knowing it really did happen in the internet dating world.

At home, he typed in lengthy notes on his meeting tonight. He would definitely be using it in his thesis. He checked his emails on Life Match to see if Rocki had sent a reply, but there wasn't one. He picked up her file and looked at her picture. Again. She was beautiful. If it weren't for the fact that he'd actually seen her at Cheesecake Factory, he would seriously be wondering if the picture was really her. But it was her. She was a gorgeous woman in the picture and in person. And he couldn't wait to meet her.

# CHAPTER 18

*T*oday was the big day. She would meet *Mr.Wrong*, Nick. It was almost nine and she was still in bed. Mainly, because she'd started thinking about having a nice hard body in her bed. Rocki kept seeing pictures of Nick's six-pack in her mind and she totally wanted to roam her hands over it. She needed to get her butt out of bed, stop thinking about sex and Nick. Especially, thinking about both sex and Nick together.

Not happening.

She got up and walked to the bathroom to take her shower. There, she could let the hot water run over her naked body and pretend the fluid movements belonged to a very hot man. Like, Nick. Damn! She actually now hoped he was ugly and such an absolute jerk, she would never want to see him again. Sadly, her gut feeling was that he was damned good looking and she would not be able to say no to him.

After she'd dressed and ate breakfast, she was ready to check her emails. First, Life Match. More emails appeared and she sighed, knowing she needed to send replies. Next, to check if she had a reply from *Mr.Right*—Dom. Yes, there was one!

*Rocki,*

*For a cold snowy Saturday night, I would grill steaks for dinner and have a glass of wine by the fire. Oh, and I can't forget to mention we would be lying on the white fur rug in front of the fireplace hopefully shedding our clothes slowly piece by piece and making love.*

*How do you feel about riding Harleys?*

*Dom*

He sounded so romantic and appeared perfectly capable of seducing her and loving her or someone, at least. Harleys? What was with these guys and their Harleys? She may have to start to like riding on motorcycles. Hell, she could get some leather chaps, a black leather jacket and boots. Maybe even a sexy black leather halter top. And she would look damn good in it, too.

*Dom,*

*Count me in for that cold snowy Saturday night! Sounds fabulously sexy and romantic.*

*Haven't been on a Harley in years, so probably need to go shopping for the appropriate leathers to wear. Shopping, I can do and do well. How do you feel about shopping?*

*Can you send a picture?*

*Rocki*

She hit send.

Now to answer some emails. She wasn't sure why but she did send a reply to *DealBreaker*, to meet him on Sunday at Starbuck's at the Village Mall for coffee.

*Gambler* wanted to meet on Monday Night. She was pretty sure that if he was an avid gambler, she definitely wouldn't be interested. At this point, she was simply playing the numbers game. You needed to meet a lot of Mr. Wrongs before you got to meet Mr. Right. It took time and effort. And she had both.

She scrolled down further and saw another email from *Mr.Wrong* —Nick. She actually hadn't expected to find one from him today since they were meeting tonight for dinner, but she noted it was from last night. Unless of course, he was cancelling. Which she doubted.

*Rocki,*

*I am looking forward to seeing you face to face.*

*Tomorrow, you meet your match.*

*Nick*

Well, he certainly had nerve that was for sure. And he was pretty damn self-assured in his ability to make her want him, when they met tonight. He seemed definitely confident he could win her over.

"We'll see." Rocki laughed.

She finished sending out emails for dates next week and went upstairs to get dressed for her afternoon meeting with *DealBreaker* —Dan.

Rocki pulled into the Village Mall's Starbucks at about two and parked. Dan was only 5'5" tall, and she liked her men taller, closer to six feet. Other than that, he looked like a nice guy. She saw he was waiting at the entrance for her as she walked in.

"Rocki, I presume," Dan said making eye contact.

"Dan?" Rocki asked.

"Yes, nice to meet you." He motioned towards the counter beside the pastry case.

They ordered coffees and macaroon muffins, then found a table where they could sit down.

Dan was the manager of a used car lot in Burnsville. He was into being suave and making deals happen. Thus, the screen name *Deal-Breaker*. Apparently, he was used to being in control of everything and everyone around him.

"You are a very beautiful woman." Dan gave her the once over with his eyes.

"Thanks," Rocki said.

Well, obviously he was interested. Unfortunately, for him, she wasn't interested at all. There were no sparks on her side. She needed to get out of there. He was a bit too much for her and she was so done with their meeting. And there wouldn't be any encores, either.

He handed her his card.

She could tell he expected her to reciprocate, but there was no way in Hell she was giving him her number.

"It was nice meeting you," Dan said as they walked out the door to the parking lot. "I'll leave it up to you, if you're interested give me a call."

"Thanks. It was nice to meet you," Rocki said.

He turned and walked away toward his car.

Rocki got in her car, thankful that date was over.

She drove home and called Allisa. "Hey, how was your date with *BikerGuy?*"

"He is a possibility. The Harley was cool. I think we both need to go shopping for biker chick outfits. Maybe, Sunday?" Allisa asked.

"I think you're right. Let's go over to the Harley store tomorrow afternoon and see what they have," Rocki suggested.

"How was your date with *HarleyGuy?*" Allisa asked.

"He was interesting. We had a nice time. Even did some slow dancing."

"Seriously? So, are you interested?" Allisa asked.

"He's a possibility. For a bad boy, that is. Not for a permanent relationship though," Rocki stated.

"Okay, so we both have at least, a possibility. Let's see how our dates go tonight and then we'll decide," Allisa suggested. "Hey, let's meet for a late breakfast at Cracker Barrel and afterwards, we can check out the Harley store for the proper attire we *will* need to go riding on these damn Harleys."

"Sounds good. I'm headed home to get ready for my date with *Mr.Wrong*—Nick."

"Great. Can't wait to hear all about it tomorrow. Have fun." Allisa ended the call.

Rocki pulled into her garage and headed up to her master bedroom to stare at the racks of clothes in her closet until she decided on something. Should she wear a dress? She wasn't sure but she wanted to look hot and show some leg, which was definitely one of her selling points. It was always the best route to take. Make a man sweat with his desire. That at least narrowed the search. She pulled out a black and gold short dress that clung to every curve of her body. And of course, the black four-inch heels. She'd picked them up off a clearance rack in the fall, because they were sandals and of course, you can't actually wear them in the winter in Minnesota.

LOOKING FOR MR. RIGHT

This would probably be a long night, so she decided to take a short nap. She laid down on the massive King-size bed and closed her eyes.

Luckily, she woke up around five, just in time to get ready for the big night. After washing her face, she applied new makeup, picked out a chunky gold tone necklace and dangly earrings to go with the dress. It would be chilly, so she chose a short light-weight black coat to wear over her dress.

She checked herself in the mirror and was pleased with what the reflection presented to her. Her long blonde hair looked slightly curled resulting in gentle waves. Sparkly gold eye shadow made her hazel eyes stand out, the dark rusty-red lipstick gave her lips a pouty look, and the dress fit her body like a glove.

About quarter after six, she was in her car and on her way to Redstone's to meet Nick. Rocki was totally unsure what the night held for her, but she was game to give it her best shot. Part of her truly wanted to hate Nick and another part wanted to love him. That way, no matter what happened she would come out a winner. It was really all just a game, so let the game begin.

She was ready.

# CHAPTER 19

*D*ominick got up early the next morning to get ready for his coffee date with *FloridaGal*, Rita. He showered and dressed quickly since he was running late. This meeting was at Dunn Brothers in Savage.

He saw her walk in while he was parking. Rita had a blonde short pixie haircut, was petite and in shape. She sold handmade shell jewelry made from the sea shells she collected on her quarterly trips to Florida. Thus, the *FloridaGal* screen name. She was waiting inside the door for him as he walked in.

"Rita?" he asked.

"Nick?" she asked.

"Yes, what would you like to drink?" he asked as they walked to the counter.

"A mocha latte, please," Rita answered.

Dominick ordered two and a couple of muffins. They picked up their drinks and sat down in chairs by the fireplace. He asked questions about her life and told her little things about himself, but mostly he asked her questions so he could use the info for his research.

"I tend to be somewhat of a free spirit and like to come and go as I please. This last winter, I decided I'd had enough of the harsh winters in Minnesota and simply packed up and headed to Florida for the entire winter," Rita said.

"I can understand not liking the winters here. They can be extremely harsh and long. It does work well for my profession of writing, though."

An hour later, they went their separate ways. Rita was a nice enough person and interesting, but he wasn't interested. No chemistry.

Dominick went home to type in his notes and to work out. Today was running on the treadmill and lifting weights. He would need another shower but that was okay. He needed to work out and this was the only time he could fit it in.

At eleven, he left to meet *YogaForLife*, Gail, at Panera in Shakopee. She only ate salads for lunch, so Panera it was. He arrived early and waited inside.

Her hair was jet black and pulled back severely in a clip on the back of her head. She was about 5'6" and had a great body, of course. Due to the yoga, he assumed.

"I'm Nick," he said walking to the door to meet her.

"Glad to meet you, Nick," she said.

They walked over to the counter to order lunch.

She picked a salad, of course, so he ordered a salad too.

"I'm assuming you like yoga," he stated.

"Yes, I'm a yoga instructor at Life Time Fitness in Savage."

They talked about what they did and what they enjoyed doing for fun. She was definitely into health foods and taking care of her body. Not that that was a bad thing, but he sensed she took it to an extreme. She was not someone he would be interested in, since she stated she was a vegetarian. He liked a great steak way too much, along with pork, ribs, ham, hamburgers, and not to leave out bacon for breakfast. No, she wasn't for him.

An hour later, they were both on their way.

Dominick went home to type in his notes and get some things

done around the house. He only had a few hours before he had another meeting.

At about two, he met *LadyGagaFan*, Lydia, at Barnes and Noble's café for coffee. He got there early and looked around at the latest new releases, so he was there when she walked in.

"Lydia?" he asked.

"Yes, you must be Nick. Glad to meet you," Lydia said.

They ordered drinks and sat down at a table to talk.

Lydia was trying to be a Lady Gaga look alike and had her hair dyed platinum blonde, was way too skinny for him and was about six feet tall, which was too tall for his liking. Although, she was definitely a striking woman and could carry on a decent conversation, she was not for him.

"So, tell me about the *LadyGagaFan* name."

"I am such a fan of Lady Gaga. I have every one of her albums. I have been to three of her concerts, even flew to New York to see one of the concerts."

"I have to be honest, I don't know much about Lady Gaga or her music."

Lydia took her phone out of her purse, scrolled down to her favorite Lady Gaga song and hit play. "Here listen, this is, *I'm on the Edge*." She tapped the speaker on so he could listen.

He listened. "Actually, I think I like it," he said, handing it back to her after the song ended. "Tell me why you like her so much."

After he had a Lady Gaga 101 lesson, where he now knew everything possible about Lady Gaga, an hour had passed and he ended the date.

He drove home and was extremely thankful *LadyBoater*, Bailey, had postponed until next week. This had allowed him to go to dinner tonight with *LoveRocks*, Rocki, instead.

He felt like a high school boy, going on his first date with a girl. Rocki was the one he'd been interested in all along and he didn't want to screw it up. No, he wanted to make a great impression. He wasn't sure he could do that as Nick, but he was certainly going to do whatever it took to make her want him. At least enough to go out on a second date.

Dominick took his time getting dressed. He picked out his black Pierre Cardin suit, with a tan shirt and matching tie with a black and gold design. His blond hair with highlights was combed back but he allowed a couple of strands to fall forward. He laughed at his appearance. "I guess, I am going for the *Thor* look, complete with blond hair and blue eyes, like Ryder said."

He picked out the Armani cologne Ryder bought him for Father's Day. She claimed it made him smell really good. He hoped she was right and Rocki would agree.

He felt bad he hadn't told Ryder he was doing the dating thing. She would've been excited for him. But she would also have wanted to give her opinion on all the women he met. Which normally would be fine, but he needed to keep his research under wraps until he was done and had enough info for the book. He would tell her later and when he seriously was dating, he would ask her opinion. Unless, of course, he found someone along the way. He was getting way ahead of the game here, this was his first date with Rocki. Best to see how it went first before making any future plans.

Dominick walked out to the garage. He was taking the Corvette tonight so he could impress Rocki. He arrived fifteen minutes early, leaving it with the valet to park. He walked inside to wait in the lobby and gave the hostess his name. He'd been told women always hated to arrive before the guy, so he always tried to be early.

Promptly at seven, the most gorgeous sexiest woman he'd ever met walked in the door. Her long blonde hair fell softly in waves, her strapless and sexy little black dress clung to her body. Every luscious curve was revealed, showing off her tan legs, arms and what could be seen of her breasts along with her flawless face. She turned his way.

"Rocki?" he asked.

"Nick," she answered.

"May I say you look absolutely ravishingly beautiful."

"Thank you," she said as a smile spread across her face and a golden hue twinkled with pleasure in her amazing hazel eyes.

"Our table is ready." He nodded to the hostess then placed his arm behind her back to escort her to the table. As he pulled the chair out for her to sit, he couldn't help but notice she had the sweetest and best ass a guy could ever ask for on a woman.

Dominick took his seat and knew—this night could change his life.

# CHAPTER 20

ocki made an on-time entrance at seven at Redstone's after parking her car herself instead of using the valet, since she had lucked out finding a parking spot right away. When she walked into the lobby and saw the gorgeous man in the black suit, her mouth almost dropped open. Then when he stood and said her name, she felt like she'd died and gone to heaven. His looks exceeded her wildest expectations. He was still a bad boy, though. She needed to keep remembering that, especially now since she'd finally met him. It was an instantaneous attraction. On her part anyway. She wasn't sure about him. But she knew it was over for her.

There was no way she would be saying no to him.

Rocki followed the waitress to their table and felt his hand gently press on her lower back to guide her. She sat down in the chair he pulled out for her. He acted like a complete gentleman and sat down across from her as she watched him intently.

The hostess handed them each a menu.

"They have great food here," Nick said. "I'm especially partial to their steaks, but the seafood is exceptional, also."

"I am thinking the Filet Mignon sounds good tonight. Nothing is better than a steak cooked to perfection," Rocki said looking up from the menu to look into his baby blue eyes that were watching her.

"Looks like we have that in common," he said.

"Yes."

"So, you consider yourself well-traveled, where is your favorite destination?" Nick asked, hoping to get her talking to him.

The waitress came to take their order.

Nick ordered a bottle of Sonoma Valley red wine.

After the waitress left, Rocki answered, "I have to say I love the clear turquoise water and white sand beaches of Cancun, especially in the winter when it's thirty below here in Minnesota."

"I have to agree with you. I've recently been to Cabo San Lucas, a few times and it has grown to quite the tourist city," Nick stated. "How about Europe?"

"I would have to say the Scandinavian countries," Rocki replied. "My grandparents were from Norway and the fjords there are totally unbelievable."

"That is one place I haven't made it to. Maybe you'll have to take me along next time you go. I actually have some great grandparents who came from Sweden and another set of grandparents who came from Iceland."

"Must be why you remind me of the guy who played Thor in the recent movie, *Thor*," Rocki said.

Nick laughed. "I hope that was a compliment."

"Of course, he's very hot," she stated matter-of-factly. "Just ask any woman."

"Well, then thank you. You have that Nordic beauty, making it obvious your ancestry is from the Scandinavian countries."

"Thank you, though the blonde hair is partially from my German heritage," Rocki stated.

"Yes, the Aryan race. I've been to Germany, have you?" Nick asked.

"I made it to Frankfurt and Munich. Got to see the Neuschwanstein Castle. They used it as an example to build the Disney Castle," Rocki stated.

"The Disney Castle in Walt Disney is remarkable. I assume you made it there?" he asked.

"A few times. Although. I like Epcot the best."

"I have to agree." Nick nodded his head. "Were you able to see the Harry Potter world they built at Universal Studios in Orlando?"

"Yes, it was absolutely incredible the detail they used to make it identical to what you have seen in the movies," Rocki said.

The waitress brought the bottle of wine and poured a sample for Nick to taste. He tasted it then nodded and she poured them each a glass.

Rocki tasted hers and was amazed at the intense taste it carried, letting everyone know it was from an excellent winery in the Napa Sonoma Valley of California.

"Tell me about your photography business," Nick said.

"I take pictures as a hobby. I am lucky with photos and have a great eye for the good shots. I sell them online though the Etsy website. I don't sell a lot, but a few sell each month."

"I'd love to see some of your photos."

"You could use a few pointers on taking pictures. The ones on your profile leave a lot to be desired," Rocki said.

"You are absolutely right," Nick agreed with a grin.

The waitress brought their food out.

"This steak is delicious," Nick stated after he cut it and took a bite. "How is your filet?"

"Very good. In fact, one of the best I've had."

Nick and Rocki concentrated on enjoying their food, leaving the conversation for later. For dessert, they ordered the Molten Chocolate cake to share.

The waitress cleared their plates and they found themselves facing each other with only their wine glasses.

Nick gave her a dazzling smile. "Do you like riding on motorcycles?"

"I guess this whole motorcycle thing is a guy thing. It's okay, I've only gone riding a few times. I think it can be a little scary," Rocki said.

"Scary? How so?" he asked.

"Well, pretty much if you fall or get hit, you're dead."

"You do have a point there, but I'm an excellent driver and if you get hit in a car you don't have any guarantees you won't be dead either, but you still drive your car."

"I suppose you're right. Do you ride a lot?" she asked.

"I drive my Corvette and my Escalade more than my Harley, so I would guess the answer would be, no?"

"Okay, I guess that was a bad question?" Rocki said laughing.

"Not necessarily. You do like riding in cars?" he asked.

"Of course. And I love Corvettes. Do you have an old classic or new one?"

"New. It's shiny, red and a convertible. I'd love to take you for a ride in it some time. Or if you prefer, we could take the Harley. Your choice," Nick offered with a wink.

"I'll take the Corvette over the Harley any day. Besides, I don't have the proper attire for the Harley."

"You mean chaps and leather jacket?" he asked.

"Yes."

"That's not a problem, I have some you could use," Nick stated.

"Are you asking me out again?" Rocki laughed, not sure what her answer would be.

"Of course, why wouldn't I?" Nick nodded his blond head. "You *are* absolutely gorgeous. I *am* attracted to you, but I'm sure that's obvious. And I *like* you. I think we could have a lot of fun together."

The waitress brought their Molten Chocolate cake out and set it on the table in front of them.

Rocki took a bite and felt heaven in her mouth, as her tongue tasted the rich molten chocolate in the center of the cake.

"Delicious," she said.

Nick took a bite after watching a look of pure pleasure wash over Rocki's face. "So, what's your answer?"

"What, was the question?" she asked.

"Would you like to go on a date and ride in my Corvette?" he asked.

LOOKING FOR MR. RIGHT

"Riding in your Corvette. . ." she repeated.

"Tomorrow around noon for brunch at Legends Golf Club?" he asked.

"Okay, I'll meet you there. And afterwards, I'll go for a ride in the Corvette," she said.

"It's a date," Nick stated simply.

"Can I trust you?" Rocki asked, searching his face in case it revealed a crazy psycho guy. But she hadn't noticed anything crazy about him. At least, not yet anyway.

~

"OF COURSE. I can't think of a reason not to trust me," Dominick said.

They finished off every last drop of the dessert.

He paid the bill and they walked into the bar section of the restaurant to listen to the band. They found one bar stool, so Rocki sat down, pulled her dress down from where it had slid up, and crossed her legs. Leaving a smooth, tan, and very bare leg for his viewing pleasure from where he stood beside the stool. The dress was low cut and from his stance, he would have a perfect view of her delectable breasts.

Dominick did so appreciate the view she was giving to him, he could even picture those tan sexy thighs wrapped around him.

The band was playing old favorites and the dance floor was full. They played a classic, *Rollin' on the River*, made famous by Tina Turner.

"Do you dance?" Dominick asked.

"Absolutely love dancing. How about you?" Rocki asked.

"Let's go." He hung his suit jacket on the back of her stool, and held out his hand.

Rocki got up off the stool and took his hand. They made their way to the dance floor, and let their bodies move in rhythm to the music. Her body swayed to the beat taking her to another place and time.

*I Will Always Love You*, from the movie, *The Bodyguard*, played next. Dominick put his arms around her waist and pulled her closer to his body. He felt her heart beating rapidly against his chest as he inhaled her Musk cologne and the sweet smell of the hairspray on her hair. Her body fit nicely against his. She was definitely a keeper. He wanted her in his bed. They had incredible chemistry on the dance floor, so he could only imagine the intensity level the sex would be at with her.

Too soon, the song ended. He took her hand and they walked back to her barstool where she took a seat. The bartender brought them refills, a coke and an ice tea, which they downed completely in minutes.

"Wow, you are a good dancer," Rocki said.

"So are you," Dominick stated.

They listened to a couple more songs and when the set ended, they walked out. Dominick walked Rocki to her car after asking the valet parking attendant get his Corvette.

Rocki stopped when she got to her car and turned to face Dominick.

He stopped abruptly, so as not to run into her and found her right up against his chest. Dominick felt hard pressed to pass up the opportunity presented to him. His arms naturally were around her in seconds, pulling her even closer against him.

Rocki leaned up to meet his lips.

Dominick kissed her deeply then ended the kiss with both of them breathless. "I'll see you at the Legends. Tomorrow. One o'clock," he said over his shoulder as he walked back to the valet stand where his Corvette was waiting. He'd played it cool but his heart was hammering in his chest.

Plus, this woman had tasted just as good as she looked.

"Yes. Tomorrow." Rocki stated and got in her car.

# CHAPTER 21

*D*ominick stepped into his Vet then observed Rocki in his rear-view mirror while she pulled out and left the parking lot. He glanced over to where the valet guys watched Rocki leave, also.

"She's one damn sexy lady," the valet said. He went silent after he sensed Nick watching him.

"Settle down boys. She's taken." Dominick gave them his menacing look to put them in their places, which definitely wasn't leering at women twice their ages, before leaving.

If the temps were a little warmer, he would've put the top down, but it remained a bit chilly this late in the evening. He was pumped. She'd met every one of his wildest expectations that a woman he chose should meet. Touching her body absolutely pushed him over the line. His hands had ever so briefly, passed over her ass, which was a definite ten. He'd felt the pressure of her breasts pushing up against his chest. He would've preferred to have her breasts in his hands, but he needed to play it cool tonight. There was always tomorrow. And the kiss was only a taste of what was to come. It was a sample, she had given freely, and he had enjoyed every minute of it.

Once home, he checked his emails. More emails to answer. First, he needed to cancel out of his morning coffee meeting with *ChevyGal* and lunch with *TopDown*. He wasn't a fan of last-minute cancellations but it was what it was and he had a much more important engagement with Rocki. He sent them each an email asking to reschedule for next week. For now, he would still plan on meeting *RedRidingHood* for dinner and *VampireQueen* later for a drink.

Now, he needed to take some notes about his date with Rocki. He began typing in the details as to the place, conversation and interaction between the two of them. The dancing and the kiss. In a way, it felt like he was betraying her, but it was only some notes about their meeting. He looked at the computer screen with its twenty plus emails waiting to be answered. They could wait until tomorrow. It was late and he wanted to get some sleep. He would be seeing Rocki tomorrow.

Dominick tried to fall asleep, but found himself lying in his King-size bed, wishing he had a warm hot-blooded female body lying next to him. Rocki. His friends told him over and over the past few years, to not worry because when it was right, he would know. Only problem was that he was supposed to be dating quite a lot of women at the present time. For the research. Mustn't forget the goal of the thesis paper. To meet many women on the internet dating site, go out on dates and keep notes.

What if Rocki really was a keeper? He had just met her as *Mr.Wrong*. He needed to play the *bad boy* part with her for at least a couple of months while he met all the other women that he would have no interest in. He was getting way ahead of himself. They hadn't even had the second date. And they hadn't slept together, yet. And he definitely wasn't making any commitments until they had.

Dominick was definitely looking forward to that test.

～

"YES. TOMORROW." Rocki had stated out loud and got in her car, before she did something totally stupid like asking him to come home with her. Damn! She badly needed a man. It had been way too long. And Nick would do very nicely.

Rocki was on cloud nine on her drive home. Her body was on fire for Nick. *The Bad Boy.* She imagined sex with him would be over the top fabulous. But of course, she shouldn't even think about having sex with him. Right? Well, that depended on what she was looking for. Unbelievable chemistry or no chemistry at all. She hadn't done that much dating after the divorce, but she knew for a fact she hadn't felt even a fraction of chemistry with the rest of the men she had met. No, they definitely didn't even come close to what she'd been looking for. Subsequently, she knew they needed to be able to get along out of bed, too.

The conversation flowed easily at dinner so she didn't think there would be any problem there. In fact, the only problem she could see so far was she would need to become accustomed to riding on a Harley and learn to enjoy it. There was little option but to give it a try since, somehow, it seemed to be a pre-requisite to dating men her age, today. She convinced herself to give it her best shot because it would be a lot of fun picking out the proper clothes.

She pulled her car into the garage and walked inside the house. She thought about checking her emails, but was way too tired and really didn't care about any of the other guys. At least, not after meeting Nick. Except maybe *Mr.Right*—Dom. She still wanted to meet him.

She went upstairs, got undressed and climbed into her big bed. Then she remembered that kiss.

There was no way she would be passing up any kisses from that man, who had already ignited her burning body with fire. She'd felt his lips branding hers with a soul searing kiss that rocked her world.

With a heavy but dreamy sigh, Rocki was asleep, only minutes later.

~

ROCKI SAT at her kitchen counter, drinking her coffee. She googled what new movies were showing at the local theaters. She wanted to find out first what kind of movies Nick liked and then maybe if he asked what she would like to do if they went out again, she could suggest a movie. Hell, here she was thinking about what they could do on a third date, when she shouldn't even be going out with him at all. Odds were that it would be fun for a while and then he would move on to the next woman on Life Match and would ultimately break her heart in the process.

Rocki was so lost in her thoughts about Nick and meeting him for brunch, she almost forgot she was supposed to meet Allisa for breakfast. She picked up her phone. "Hey, you up Allisa?" Rocki wondered if her friend had still been sleeping.

"Just got up. What's going on?" Allisa asked.

"I can't meet you for breakfast because I'm having brunch with Nick at Legends," Rocki stated. "How about I meet you after at the Harley store?"

"What time do you think you'll be done?"

"Probably can meet you at four. If I get done earlier, I'll call you."

"Okay, I've got a dinner date at seven, so we should be fine," Allisa said. "Call me when you're done, I'll be here."

"Sounds good. Then you can tell me all about your date last night, too."

"And I need to hear about yours, as well." Allisa disconnected the call.

Rocki hadn't showered yet because she wanted to work out first, so up to the workout room first. Then the shower.

At noon, Rocki was dressed in a perky peach-print sundress with matching heeled sandals in peach. She was ready. The temperature was supposed to reach seventy today, so she should be dressed appropriately.

It looked like a beautiful sunny day. Rocki felt happy today as she pulled into the parking lot.

Nick's Corvette was parked off to the side where he was lounging with his shoulder leaning against the side of the club building. When he saw her walking towards him, he smiled. "Rocki, I've been waiting for you. Seems like a lifetime." He embraced her with a full hug and a quick short kiss on the lips.

"Nick. It's been less than twelve hours," Rocki said.

With that gorgeous smile, he swung his arm around her lower back and escorted her inside.

It had been a long time since she'd felt this at ease with a man. Just something about him made her feel comfortable.

They were escorted to a table by the window, overlooking the golf course. It presented massive views of already lush green grass and a water pond with a water fountain in the center spraying arcs of water in an umbrella shape.

They decided on the buffet and made their way up to fill their plates with all the delicious entrees and side dishes.

"Have you been here before?" Nick asked after they sat down with their plates.

"Once, for a luncheon with some girlfriends," Rocki replied. "How about you?"

"It's a great golf course and I'm a member here," he said. "Do you golf?"

"Yes, I haven't golfed for a couple of years now, but I used to be on a ladies golf league," she stated.

"Maybe we'll have to go golfing? I belong to the Wilds Golf Club, too."

"I'm sure you're a much better golfer than I am. Are you sure you can golf with a beginner?" Rocki teased.

"Not a problem. Maybe I can give you some pointers," he replied.

"So do you do indoor sports?"

Nick smiled. "What did you have in mind?"

Rocki shook her head as a smile spread across her face. "Get your mind out of the gutter. I meant like going to see a movie."

"Yes, I watch movies, if that is what you're asking." He gave her that cute grin of his.

"Good. What kind of movies do you like?"

"I like Sci-Fi, Action Adventure, and Murder Suspense," Nick said.

"Oh. . .I didn't hear Romantic Comedies," she prodded smiling.

"You mean Chic Flicks. I've been known to watch a couple every once in a while. Usually, the *Chics* are pretty hot which can make the whole movie worthwhile." He continued grinning.

"Hey, that works for me. How you make it through the whole movie, makes no difference. As long as you watch the whole thing, so we can have an in-depth conversation about the story and plot line afterwards," she teased as she tried not to laugh but didn't succeed.

When they finished breakfast, they walked out on the patio.

"Ready to let me take you for the ride of your life?" Nick asked as he put his arm around her waist.

Rocki turned to face him. "Ride of my life, huh? Have at it. I'm all yours," she added as a sly smile crossed her lips.

Nick chuckled as he took her hand and led her out to the parking lot to his shiny red Corvette. He opened the door and she stepped inside while he walked around to his side and got in. Engine on, seat belts on, and they were on their way. The roads nearby were old farm roads and had very little traffic. The Corvette practically flew down the road. The farms with cows and fields were flying by as the car accelerated.

$\sim$

Pulling into Cleary Lake Reserve, he parked away from all the other cars. He then came around to open her door and help her out. They walked down to the shoreline of the lake where the sun glistened on the water and the waves rolled gently toward shore.

He took her hand in his and they walked slowly down the beach. "So why are you on Life Match, Rocki?"

"Didn't think the odds were in my favor that my *Knight in Shining Armor* would just walk up to my door and ring the bell."

"Well put," he said. "So, how is Life Match working out for you?"

"It's only been a week. Everyone has been interesting, I will say," Rocki offered.

"Any keepers?"

"Not sure yet," Rocki said.

"So, what is a key factor in finding a keeper, according to Rocki?"

Rocki remained silent for a moment. "Chemistry and intense passion."

"I'll second that," Dominick said.

They were back to where the car was parked now.

Dominick leaned against the Vet with his back and turned Rocki into his arms. His lips were on hers and her breasts were pressing against his chest. He kissed her long and hard. His body was on fire. He wanted to undress her slowly and make love to every inch of her body in his bed.

Unfortunately, asking her to come home with him today was totally out of the question.

"We definitely have the chemistry." Dominick moved them both away from the car and opened the door for her to get in. He went around the car to get in and they were back at Legends in a few minutes.

Dominick walked Rocki to her car. He took her in his arms again and gave her a warm but quick kiss. "Can I interest you in a movie on Thursday night? I'll even let you pick the movie."

Rocki hesitated only a moment. "Yes."

# CHAPTER 22

On Dominick's drive home, all he could think about was kissing Rocki and all the other things he'd like to do to her body. He had absolutely no desire to meet these other women today, but it was for his research. The Thesis. Which is what the whole thing was about. It wasn't about finding a woman to spend the rest of his life with. That was what people say though—when you're not looking...it will just happen. He would have to be careful, though, if she actually ended up being his soul mate. There was a strong chance she would turn and run once she found out he'd lied to her. Lying was such a bad way to start a relationship.

Hopefully, this would all work out in the end.

Once he arrived home, he typed up his notes about their date, then sent out more emails to potential matches, setting up meeting times. This whole dating thing was really becoming extremely time consuming and now he needed to set aside some time for Rocki, too. Which reminded him he needed to send out return emails to *Mr.Right's* potential matches. He found it odd that only one of the *Mr.Wrong's* matches had emailed both his *Mr.Wrong* and *Mr.Right* profiles, besides Rocki. He also needed to send her a return email as *Mr.Right* to the email she'd sent.

*Dom,*

*Count me in for that cold snowy Saturday night! Sounds fabulously sexy and romantic.*

*Haven't been on a Harley in years, so probably need to go shopping for the appropriate leathers to wear. Shopping I can do and do well. How do you feel about shopping?*

*Can you send a picture?*

*Rocki*

He would love to see her in skin tight leather chaps and a sexy little leather top, designed to reveal cleavage. Whoever designed those tops certainly knew how to get a man's attention. That was for sure.

*Rocki,*

*Shopping isn't a guy thing, but I have been known to go shopping with a woman on rare occasions. And shopping for appropriate leathers would certainly qualify as a justifiable rare occasion.*

*Been busy with work stuff, so haven't had a chance to post any new pictures. On my list though.*

*Do you like to watch movies? What is your favorite movie of all time?*

*Dom*

Dominick hit send. He really wanted to send her an email from Nick, but didn't want to seem overly eager, so he would wait. She hadn't offered her phone number yet, but then again, he hadn't asked for it either. He would ask her for one of her photography business cards on Thursday.

Dominick finished up some projects around the house, and then headed over to Chili's in Shakopee to meet *RedRidingHood*, Red. Flaming red hair down to the middle of her back was the basis for her nickname, Red. She was an attractive woman about 5'5" with a great body, although a little bit too much on the thin side for his liking. Red was the production manager for Chanhassen Dinner Theater and had done quite a bit of acting through the years. She was lively and the conversation about all the different things that happened behind the curtain of shows was extremely entertaining.

They had no chemistry but it was a pleasant dinner.

He stopped at the local Home Depot to check out some new items for the patio he had seen in the advertisement flyer of the local newspaper.

At seven, he drove to Outback in Burnsville to meet *VampireQueen*, Mira. He had to admit he felt a little leery about meeting her. He really didn't get into the vampire stuff. Obviously, she had picked that as her name, so probably meant she was into it way too much. He walked in and saw a lady with long black hair, dressed completely in black with very pale white skin and knew it had to be Mira.

She turned his way and smiled as he walked to the bar. "Hi, I'm Mira. Hope it's okay to sit at the bar," she said.

Dominick took a seat on the barstool next to her as he nodded and said, "I'm Nick."

The bartender took their order for a couple of beers on tap and set them on the counter within a few moments.

"So, tell me about the *VampireQueen* name," he said, curiosity almost getting the best of him. Hell, she was probably into kinky sex. Might be interesting to try. Once. But then again, maybe not. She seemed a bit too strange for him.

Red told him about all the vampire books and the fan clubs that had started up recently. They even had meetings where everyone could dress up as vampires and the only beverage served was a drink mixture of cranberry juice, red wine and cream to thicken it, so it kind of looked like blood. They wore fang caps on their teeth to make them look more like vampires. Sex with multiple partners was an accepted thing in the club.

She'd designed the website for the Vampire Club and it had taken off to the point, that it was her job to maintain it now. She collected membership dues from members and set up the monthly parties down in Stillwater at a restaurant that was part of the old St. Croix River caves. *What an appropriate location.*

"Here's my card with the website info. If you want to stop by one of the events anytime, call or email me and I will put you on the guest list," Red said.

"Thanks. I'll let you know," he said.

After they finished their beers, he said goodbye and headed home.

Dominick was actually a little shocked to think this sort of thing really went on, especially in Minneapolis. She definitely did not interest him and he supposed the reason she had emailed him was because she figured a bad boy would be into kinky sex with almost anyone. Not him. But it definitely would make interesting reading in his thesis.

After he arrived home, he immediately typed in notes about Red and her Vampire Club. He certainly would be using some of this information in his thesis.

Pulling up his calendar for next week, he took a look at his schedule. He was only going to have three meetings a day since he'd made some cancellations because of Rocki. Their date today and then the date on Thursday night with her would mean he needed to rearrange others and probably would have to do four a day. This was getting old fast.

He was meeting, *BlackWidow*, Monday morning at Starbucks. *KarateKid*, for lunch at O'Malley's in Prior Lake, *ShadyLady* at Bogart's in Apple Valley for a drink after work. Then he rescheduled *Chevy-Lady* for dinner at Olive Garden.

On Tuesday, he had *RubySlippers* for coffee at Caribou. *Twister* for lunch at Panera in Apple Valley, and *Librarian* for a drink after work at Wild Bills in Apple Valley. And he'd rescheduled *TopDown* for supper at Bucca's in Burnsville.

Wednesday, he had *OliveOil* for coffee at Dunn Brothers Coffee Shop, *Goldie* for lunch at Noodles in Burnsville. *SalsaQueen* for dinner and drinks after work at Theresa's in Lakeville.

Thursday, he was meeting *ChurchLady* for coffee at Starbucks in Savage. *DodgeGirl* for lunch at Lion's Tap in Eden Prairie, and the evening was for Rocki.

Friday, he had coffee in the morning with *DreamGirl* at Caribou's, *DiamondGirl* for lunch at Champs in Burnsville. Then he would leave Friday night open for Rocki. Just in case, he needed it.

It wasn't as many dates as he'd had the week before but it would be sufficient for his research. During that time, he would figure the whole thing out with Rocki to see if he wanted to take it further. Meaning…to see if he really was ready to give his heart away again.

Dominick knew that he needed to find out if he actually wanted to give it to her.

# CHAPTER 23

$\mathcal{R}$ocki called Allisa from her car as she drove to the Harley store. "I'm on my way. I should be right on time."

"Good, I'll leave now." Allisa pressed end call on her phone screen.

Minutes later, they both pulled into the parking lot of the Harley store in Lakeville. They walked in together and were greeted by a sales girl.

"I'm interested in getting some leather chaps and a jacket," Rocki stated.

They were led to the back of the store where the women's apparel was located. Then they began their search for the perfect leather jacket and chaps that fit exactly right.

An hour later and right before closing, Rocki purchased leather chaps, a T-shirt with a Harley logo on the front, a black leather jacket, a pair of boots, a purse and a pair of glasses that would stay on while riding. Oh, and a leather strap that snapped around her long hair once it was in a ponytail to keep it from becoming *one big snarled mess*, as the sales girl put it. She was now set to go riding on a Harley. Nick's Harley. She just hoped it didn't scare her to death once she was on it. Men! They weren't happy unless there were risks involved. But she wasn't so sure just being able to stay alive was a risk she wanted to take. Especially over and over and over again.

Allisa had a little time before her dinner date and they stopped at Starbucks for coffee so they could talk.

"You must like this Nick if you went out and spent a fortune on an outfit to go riding with him," Allisa stated the obvious.

"Oh my God!" Rocki exclaimed. "The chemistry is unreal. And his kisses. Boy, does he know how to kiss!"

"O-kay. But he's the *bad boy* one, right?" Allisa asked.

"I know. That's the tricky part. He makes me feel so comfortable when I'm around him."

"Are you going to sleep with him?" Allisa asked.

"I know I really shouldn't even be thinking about it, but. . .I want to," Rocki stated.

"Do you think he just does one-night stands?" Allisa asked.

"I don't know. Right now, though, I think it would be worth taking a chance even to have one night of unbelievable great sex. It's been a long time," Rocki professed.

"If you are sure, you won't fall apart when he dumps you for his next conquest, I say go for it. You've never done anything like this before. You played by the rules last time and it still got you a broken heart, so what the heck?"

They finished their coffees, and Allisa took off to meet her date for dinner at Bucca's.

Rocki went home with all her new purchases. Once she was home, she tried on the complete biker chic outfit. She looked at herself in the mirror and saw a completely hot sexy chic in the mirror. It was so surreal she couldn't believe it was actually her. Just goes to show what the right clothes can do to change who you are into who you could be.

After she changed back into jeans, she checked her emails. She needed to get her schedule straight for next week.

Luckily, *DealBreaker*, had not responded earlier, because she'd totally forgotten she was supposed to meet him for coffee this morning. He'd sent an email this afternoon, apologizing for not checking his emails earlier and wanted to reschedule for next week Tuesday.

She sent a reply, accepting his dinner invitation at Red Lobster in Burnsville.

*Gambler* had replied and wanted to meet her at Mystic Lake Casino for dinner at their new restaurant, Primo, at seven on Monday night.

*CaptainJack* wanted to meet on Wednesday night for dinner at none other than Captain Jack's on Prior Lake. This seemed a little too ironic, but it was close by. It should be interesting anyway, so she accepted.

Thursday was her date with Nick. She needed to check what movies were showing again and pick one for them to see. He liked Sci-Fi, so she chose the new Marvel movie.

She scrolled down through the emails and found one from *Mr.Right*. Damn, but she still wanted to meet him. He seemed so perfect for her.

*Rocki,*

*Shopping isn't a guy thing, but I have been known to go shopping with a woman on rare occasions. And shopping for appropriate leathers would certainly qualify as a justifiable rare occasion.*

*Been busy with work stuff, so haven't had a chance to post any new pictures. It is on my list though.*

*Do you like to watch movies? What is your favorite movie of all time?*

*Dom*

Well, too late for the shopping part, she'd already taken care of that. He must really be busy if he can't even manage to post a picture and she had to wonder if he actually wanted to meet anyone because she couldn't imagine any woman agreeing to meet him without seeing a picture first. She needed to get him to post a picture or send one before this really went any further because they wouldn't be going anywhere together without the picture.

*Dom,*

*Really need to see the picture before this can proceed much further. Not that looks are everything, but everyone has to like what they see.*

*I love movies. Suspense, Adventure, Romance. How about you?*

*How often do you ride your Harley?*

*Rocki*

She hit send. If he didn't send a picture soon or post one, she didn't think she should spend any more time emailing with him.

She went back to refresh her email section in Life Match, and sure enough there was one from Nick.

*Rocki,*

*I enjoyed your company today.*

*Did you pick a movie for Thursday?*

*Nick*

It dawned on her that she hadn't given him her phone number, so he couldn't call her.

She typed a reply to his short email.

*Nick,*

*You certainly know how to show a girl a good time.*

*My movie choice would be the new Marvel movie. I'm sure you will love it.*

*See you, Thursday.*

*Rocki*

Well, that was enough emails for today. She was leaving Friday open in case she wanted to go out with Nick again.

If he asked, of course.

It had been a long week full of surprises. Some good and some not so good. Tonight, she was going to sit down, take it easy and catch up on watching some of her Hallmark movies. Yes, that sounded like a great idea.

Monday at work, Rocki told her co-workers about her not one but *two* dates with Nick. They were ecstatic when she told them he'd kissed her more than once. The day flew by and before she knew it, the work day was over. She stopped home to change quickly before meeting *Gambler*, Gabe, at Mystic Lake Casino.

She walked in and headed toward the Ticket Box office where she was meeting him. He stood there waiting as she walked up. Gabe was not bad looking at all. At about 5'10", with coal black hair and brown eyes, he was dressed in most likely designer jeans and a black pinstriped button-down shirt. Too bad, he was more than likely a gambler.

They walked down the corridor that led to the other part of the casino where the new restaurant was located. It was catering to the fine dining clientele, probably their high rollers. They were shown a table almost immediately. But of course, it was Monday, after all.

They ordered lobster and steak dinners.

Gabe explained that he was a professional gambler.

She didn't think people actually did that for a living. Of course, she'd seen the shows on TV, but really hadn't thought they had any of them in the Twin Cities. It was interesting to learn about what he did, but he definitely wasn't for her. And oddly enough, even though he was quite good looking, she felt no chemistry.

After arriving home, she saw a reply email from Nick.

*Rocki,*

*You make it easy.*

*New Marvel movie it is.*

*Meet me at five at Harry's across from the Lakeville theaters and we'll have a bite to eat before the movie.*

*See you at five on Thursday.*

*Nick*

That would work out just fine!

Tuesday after work, she met *DealBreaker*, Del, at Red Lobster. A used car salesman thru and thru. She ordered shrimp this time. He was about 5'6", with brown short hair and hazel eyes. Not bad looking, but he did nothing to undo the sleazy, slimy used car salesman visual, she'd harbored for years.

Wednesday after work, she met *CaptainJack*, Jack, at Captain Jack's on the lake. Jack stood about 5'11" with a short, grey spiked hair cut with blue eyes. He was actually very attractive. Jack turned out to be a real Captain Jack...a pilot for Delta Airlines. He had great stories to tell about flying and things that actually happened on the planes.

Rocki thought she could possibly like him. A slight spark fired between them, but unfortunately, it was nothing compared to what she felt for Nick. Although, she would consider going on a second date with him in case it didn't work out with Nick. What was she thinking? There simply wasn't any possibility that it would work out with Nick. At least, not long term anyway. Jack was nice and she didn't want to burn any bridges she might be interested in for later. So, if he asked, she would go out with him again.

On her way home, all she could think about was her date with Nick tomorrow night. Earlier in the week, he'd emailed and asked if she wanted to have a bite to eat first at Harry's across the street from the Lakeville Movie theaters. Rocki accepted but wasn't so sure she'd get any sleep tonight. She was way too excited to see Nick again.

Now, if only she knew if he was excited, too.

# CHAPTER 24

First thing in the morning, Dominick checked his emails and found one from Rocki to *Mr.Right*.

*Dom,*

*Really need to see the picture before this can proceed much further. Not that looks are everything, but everyone has to like what they see.*

*I love movies. Suspense, Adventure, Romance. How about you?*

*How often do you ride your Harley?*

*Rocki*

He wasn't sure how much longer he could lead her on without a picture. But he was going to try as long as he could.

*Rocki,*

*I am hoping to have some free time this weekend, so I can get a picture taken that looks decent and post it.*

*Do you like James Bond movies?*

*As for the Harley, I usually go riding whenever the weather permits in the late spring, summer and early fall. I'd love to take you riding.*

*Dom*

He scrolled down further and saw one from Rocki to *Mr.Wrong*.

*Nick,*

*You certainly know how to show a girl a good time.*

*My movie choice would be the new Marvel movie. I'm sure you will love it.*

*See you, Thursday.*

*Rocki*

Wow, he hadn't expected her praise at all. He couldn't wait to see her Thursday.

*Rocki,*

*You make it easy.*

*New Marvel movie it is.*

*Meet me at five at Harry's across from the Lakeville theaters and we'll have a bite to eat before the movie.*

*See you at five on Thursday.*

*Nick*

Monday morning at nine, Dominick arrived at Starbucks to meet *BlackWidow*, Lucinda. A tall, black beauty and an absolutely breathtaking widow, dressed completely in black with a veil over her face.

Just a bit over the top for him.

He met *KarateKid*, Kate, for lunch at O'Malley's. She was a karate instructor with a black belt. He certainly wouldn't want to take her on in a fight.

Nice lady but not for him.

Later at five thirty, he met *ShadyLady*, Shayla, at Bogart's for a drink. She was an energetic lady who had a window treatment business. A petite woman with shoulder length blunt-cut brunette hair.

Nice person, but no chemistry at all, so not for him.

Promptly as seven, he met *ChevyLady*, Cheryl, a tall thin lady with strawberry blonde hair to her shoulders. She was into cars, especially Chevys. Surprise, surprise. She knew everything anyone could possibly need or want to know about Camaros and Corvettes. She owned a '69 Z-28 and was in charge of a local Camaro club. Extremely sexy lady.

He almost wished he felt some chemistry, but it wasn't there.

Dominick finally made it home about nine. It had been a long day on the job. Yes, that was what he was doing—working. He spent an hour typing in his notes on each date and then crashed in bed.

~

TUESDAY MORNING, Dominick was at Caribou to meet *RubySlippers*, Ruby. She stood at about 5'8", trim and fit body, with brown shoulder length hair and green eyes. She owned a novelty store, carrying movie classic paraphernalia and she knew practically all the movie facts about all the classics. The conversation proved extremely interesting and entertaining.

Now if only he could remember some of the movie facts so he could impress Rocki on Thursday.

For lunch, he met *Twister*, Teri, who worked in the weather room on Channel 5 and was one of the people who tracked storms. He learned things he never knew about the weather. Teri was an attractive tall and slender woman with platinum blonde long hair.

A nice person, but no chemistry.

At five, he met the *Librarian*, Lina, at Wild Bill's in Apple Valley for a drink. Lina in no way resembled the librarian stereo type. A vivacious 5'6" woman with dark brown, long hair and brown eyes. Oh, and no glasses. She actually was a librarian, but her passion was searching for lost treasures, like the movie series, *The Librarian*.

Intriguing woman but not for him.

A couple of hours later, Dominick met *TopDown*, Tori, for dinner at Bucca's in Burnsville. A petite, brunette with chin length hair and hazel eyes. Tori just plain loved convertibles and would love to go for a ride in his Corvette. She was a basic *air head* which made conversation extremely trying to say the least and he was relieved when it was finally over.

Finally, the day was over and he was home typing his notes in the computer. Another long day, he thought, as he climbed into bed. At least now, he could close his eyes and think about Rocki.

Wednesday morning found Dominick at Dunn Brothers Coffee to meet *OliveOil*, Livey, who was a chef at Macaroni Grill in Edina. Livey was originally from England and still had a British accent.

A very nice lady but not for him.

For lunch, he met *Goldie*, Edie, at Noodles at the Burnsville Center.

A brunette with brown eyes and the manager of a jewelry store, The Gold Store. She had a zest for life, evident from the stories she told him about all the things she did in her spare time.

He didn't think he could keep up with her and it would drive him crazy trying.

Later for dinner, he met *SalsaQueen*, Sasha, at Theresa's in Lakeville. Part Latin and an experienced Salsa Dancer, she embraced her heritage by running the Mexican restaurant, Theresa's, where they were dining. She also spoke Spanish fluently. Her long black hair framed her lovely face and dark eyes. Her body was everything a man could ask for.

He wouldn't fit into her world well at all and the chemistry wasn't there.

Finally, he was home, typing in notes on all his dates. It had been a long day, but he had met some very diverse women, all with different agendas in mind. Each one had their own unique story to tell. After he typed in notes on a date, he printed it out and made a file with their name on it. At the end of each date, he asked for their business card and if it didn't have a phone number or email, he asked them to write it on the back of the card. If they didn't have a card, although most did, he had them write the info on the back of one of his cards. He had special cards made up with Nick Sager, a P.O Box number and the email he had set up especially for the internet dates. He hadn't given Rocki a card yet, seeing how he had been too preoccupied with kissing her. So tomorrow night, he would give her one, only on hers he would put his cell phone number. He wanted her to be able to call him. He went to bed tonight with a smile, knowing tomorrow night, he would see Rocki.

Dominick met *ChurchLady*, Cheri, at Starbuck's the next morning at nine. She was about 5'5" with dirty blonde, curly, chin length hair and blue eyes. She was an actress in the Basement Church Ladies play, currently showing at the Plymouth Playhouse Theater.

Interesting lady but not for him.

He drove home and set to work in his office, typing in his notes from his date that morning.

About eleven thirty, he took the Corvette and headed to Lion's Tap to meet *DodgeGirl* for lunch. At about 5'7", average figure, reddish brown hair, with green eyes, Dodi, was an auto mechanic. Boy, she really knew her cars and was a huge Dodge fan. She drove a new style Cuda, bright orange with a 455 engine.

Nice girl but too much of a tomboy for him.

Rapidly, typing in his notes on the date after arriving home, he worked on an outline for the book he was writing for publication, loosely based on the results of the online dating process which would be used for his thesis. It would be a uniquely interesting and intriguing story, he had no doubt. In fact, he had high hopes it would become a bestseller like his other books. He had quite a bit of information already, but he needed more. About two more weeks' worth of date evaluations should do it. At least, he hoped so, because to be perfectly frank, he was tired of going on dates. Almost all the women did nothing for him, as far as piquing his interest.

Except for one…Rocki.

Dominick changed into the fancy designer, dark blue jeans, Ryder had picked out for him along with a new in-style designer shirt, she'd also picked out. He couldn't wait to see Rocki, again and the Corvette would be the vehicle of choice tonight. Mostly, he wanted to kiss her. Again. Unfortunately, what he really desired was to get her into his bed, but he wasn't sure how he could make that happen.

First, he'd have to convince her it was perfectly safe to come to his house. Women were so careful these days with all the crap happening that he wouldn't blame her for being cautious. In fact, she had every reason to be careful, especially after a woman was recently killed by a man who answered a posting on Tinder's hook up site. And she hadn't lived very far from Prior Lake. About the only way he could succeed would be to get her so turned on by his kisses that she would be overcome with such strong desire for him that she would desperately want to finish what they'd started.

Most likely, it wouldn't happen tonight, but he would work on it tomorrow night.

Dominick left in the Corvette and headed to Harry's to meet Rocki for appetizers. He'd been anticipating that the movie would be great, because he liked super-hero themed movies, subsequently it should be a good night. He wanted nothing more than to be in her good graces, so an action-packed movie it was. Which also meant he could enjoy her company for the entire evening.

About fifteen minutes early, he pulled into the parking lot and parked the Corvette in a back corner, where he hoped no one would ding the doors. He walked in and got a table, because he knew the place soon would be full with the whole after work group of customers who were probably regulars. He waited patiently but kept one eye on the door.

Rocki walked in promptly at five.

# CHAPTER 25

Rocki brought her jeans and sexy top to change into after work, so she could get to Harry's by five. She usually got done work at four-thirty, so a few minutes before then, she slipped into the bathroom to change, freshen up her makeup, and spray on some fresh cologne. She wanted to smell good for Nick, she thought, adjusting her V-neck top to show a little more cleavage. *What am I doing?* She realized just how much she wanted him to want her. Hell, she wanted him to kiss her again, so she definitely intended to appear inviting. *What is going on with me?* She was sorely tempting a bad boy to have his way with her, as they say.

Yes, she was and she no longer cared if he was a bad boy or not.

About five, she pulled into Harry's parking lot and saw his Corvette parked in a corner spot in the back, so she knew he was already inside waiting. She parked and walked in. Her dark blue jeans fit like a glove, her black V-neck knit top hugged her body. The boots were black with three-inch heels which made her appear taller. Nick was six feet tall, so she would still be shorter than him.

As soon as she entered, she saw him at a table near the window. He'd probably been watching her as she walked in, she thought. She went over to his table and sat down on a chair across from him.

"You look great," he complimented.

"Thanks," Rocki said.

He handed her the appetizer menu with the happy hour specials to look over. They decided to order wings and deep-fried spiral cut potatoes along with Cokes.

"So how was your day today?" he asked.

"Oh, just the usual. I do get to take some pictures at an event tomorrow night, so that is exciting. Every once in a while, they let me shoot some photos that actually go in the newspaper."

"What's the event?"

"Actually, a birthday party. The paper needs photos for an article about the old Larson farm. So, I'll be taking photos of the house, barn and acreage. Then there will be a 95$^{th}$ birthday party for old man Larson at the Community Center, where they will be interviewing him."

"Sounds like a good time. Those old guys can sometimes be a wealth of very interesting information," he said.

The waitress brought their drinks and food.

"That was quick." Rocki was hungry and began eating.

"They try to get the food out fast because they know a lot of people in here are trying to make it to a movie." He picked up a wing and started eating.

"How was your day?" Rocki asked, realizing she only knew he was a writer, according to his profile. Her curiosity about this man and his life was now peaking high.

"Kept busy doing some research for a project I'm doing for a client."

Rocki took note that he didn't want to talk much about his work, so she changed the subject, "I've heard this new Marvel movie is quite good. You've seen the others, right?"

"Of course, but it was a while ago. I did hear this one outdoes the others."

"Yes, not sure how they do it but it always seems like the new movie is better than the previous one," Rocki stated.

"So do I get to pick the movie next time?" He watched her closely.

Rocki was secretly thrilled. Yes, another date! "Fine, as long as it isn't a horror movie. I just can't watch them because I'd probably have to close my eyes for 95% of the movie."

He laughed. "I promise not to pick a Horror movie."

They finished eating and drove across the street in his Corvette, leaving her car at Harry's. She assumed it would be okay, knowing her car was across the street if she needed it for some odd reason. Why she was thinking this, she had no idea because she felt perfectly safe with Nick.

They walked into the theater and were excited that it was showing on the monster screen. The wonderful smell of buttered popcorn was way too good to pass by, so they purchased two small popcorns and two sodas. He'd purchased tickets online, so they went in to find their reclining seats in the middle of the row towards the top and sat down.

Rocki reclined her chair, got comfy in the seat next to Nick who seemed to be enjoying the movie previews. While they watched the movie, they managed to finish off their popcorns even though they'd just eaten.

After the movie, they walked out to Nick's car and got in.

He drove across the street to where her car was parked. "I'd like to take you riding on Saturday. There's a biker rally in Mankato. It's not that far and would be a good way for you to try it out and see if you like it or not. I have some leathers that will fit you," he said.

"What time would we leave?" she asked.

"Eleven. It takes about an hour to get down there. The weather is supposed to be great—clear and 75 degrees."

"I have chaps and a jacket," she said.

"Okay. So, you'll give the Harley a try?"

"What time will we be back?" Rocki asked.

"Probably by five."

"Okay, I'll try it," Rocki said.

"Here's my card with my personal email and phone. Do you want me to pick you up or meet me at my house?" Nick asked.

Rocki stopped to think about it for a minute. She wasn't so sure she wanted him to know where she lived yet, but she wasn't sure she wanted to go to his house either. She knew those were the choices and she needed to pick one. "I'll drive over to your house."

"Here, I'll put my address on the back of my card." Nick held his hand out for her to place the card in his palm. He quickly wrote down his address and handed her back the card.

Rocki slid it into her purse. She would Google the address to get directions, later. He stepped out of the car and walked to her side to open the door. Rocki got out. Nick shut the door and stood in front of her. Before she knew it, she was in his arms and her body was pressed against his with his lips on hers for a hot, spellbound kiss that knocked her for a loop.

The kiss ended almost as swiftly as it began.

He took her hand and walked toward her car. "I'll see you Saturday. Have a good time tomorrow night at the birthday party." He gave her a wickedly sexy smile that promised all sorts of mischievous things.

Rocki slipped into her car, while watching Nick walk away toward his Corvette. She drove home in a glorious haze. His kisses simply ignited all her emotions. They rocked her world, in a good way. She loved them. Not him, but the kisses. It was too soon to love him, right?

She told her phone to call Allisa.

"Rocki. How'd the movie date go?"

"Allisa, do you think you can fall in love with someone in three dates?" Rocki asked.

"What? Wow! You really like this guy, don't you?" Allisa questioned.

"He's so damn hot. And there is definitely chemistry!"

"But remember, he's the bad boy. It's a little soon to be talking about the *Love* word."

"I know. I'm sure it's just an infatuation with wanting what you know isn't good for you," Rocki stated.

"Good. You were scaring me there for a minute." Allisa sighed heavily into the phone.

"But I did agree to go to a biker rally in Mankato on Saturday with him and ride on his Harley."

"Good thing you bought the leather outfit," Allisa said.

"He gave me his address and I am meeting him at his house Saturday morning," Rocki added.

"It will be interesting to see what his house is like," Allisa commented.

"I know. I am curious. I never asked him anything about where he lived and he never said anything, so I have no clue what it will be like. I'll do a map quest for the directions tomorrow. I'm too tired to do it tonight."

"Well in case you're interested," Allisa stated. "My date tonight was definitely not a keeper. Total weirdo. Talked like he grew up in the backwoods or something like that. Although I have to say, the one for tomorrow night sounds promising, so we'll see."

"Okay, good luck. Let me know tomorrow, how it goes," Rocki said.

"Oh, the movie! How was it?" Allisa asked.

"They did an excellent job on the special effects. Loved it."

"Okay, I'll call you tomorrow night after my date." Allisa ended the call.

Rocki pulled in her garage and walked into her house. It had been a long day and she was tired. She intended to go to bed as soon as possible.

Half an hour later, she was in bed and fell asleep almost instantly, thinking about the unbelievable kiss from Nick. It made her body involuntarily arc toward his body. Well, at least her body knew what it wanted even though her head wasn't sure.

Unlike all the other men she'd been dating...the chemistry between her and Nick was off the charts.

# CHAPTER 26

*ominick* was pleased with the progression of his relationship with Rocki. Saturday would be the big night. Hopefully, anyway. After they drove back from Mankato, he would invite her in for a glass of wine and dinner or they could order a pizza. He didn't actually care as long she was inside his house, relaxed, and turned on so she would consider taking the walk upstairs to his master bedroom. Yes, he was looking forward to finding out where this unbelievable chemistry could take them.

He couldn't wait.

Friday morning, he was off to meet *DreamGirl*, Deanna, at Caribou Coffee. She was already there when he arrived early. A laptop rested on the table in front of her where she'd probably been working on something. She stood at about six feet tall, black hair with a couple of purple streaks and blue eyes. Pretty face and nice body. Her jewelry business featured handcrafted designs she'd made. To market her jewelry, she participated in craft shows all across the U.S. and supplied a couple of boutique stores with her jewelry. Nice person but she was a bit too dreamy, for lack of a better word, and a free spirit.

No, not for him.

Dominick stopped home to type in his notes while they were still fresh in his mind and answered some emails to potential matches. He set up appointments for next week during the daytime, and deliberately left the evenings open for Rocki. Once they had sex, they would be an item which meant they hopefully would be having sex often. Knowing how intense their chemistry was it would most likely be as often as possible. That was, if he had anything to say about it.

At one, he met *DiamondGirl*, Amanda, at Champs in Burnsville for lunch. She was about 5'4", with golden blonde hair and hazel eyes. She managed a Jared's jewelry store, knew everything about diamonds and where they came from. Needless to say, she was all decked out in diamonds—earrings, necklace, bracelets, and rings. All done in good taste, though, not gaudy. Very classy lady and he wouldn't mind seeing more of her, if it didn't work out with Rocki.

However, Dominick felt quite confident his relationship with Rocki would work out and would most likely exceed his wildest expectations.

He took Amanda's card, walked with her to the parking lot, then headed home to type in more notes. Sitting at his desk, he realized he still hadn't received a reply to the email he sent Rocki from *Mr.Right*. Maybe, he'd kept her too busy. He'd been looking forward to not having any dates tonight so he could work out and catch up on some of his shows. There was always something good on the Discovery or History Channel. He liked watching them because they always provided good information that he might need to use in a book someday.

At ten, he turned on the news and caught a short clip about the Larson farm and Gunnar Larson's 95th birthday. He actually thought he glimpsed a woman who looked like Rocki in the background. Possibly, could be her since she was there. He absolutely knew he would be dreaming about her as soon as he fell asleep.

～

ROCKI HAD a busy day at work getting ready for the Larson birthday party event where she'd been designated to be the photographer. She felt excited because it was a chance to do what she actually liked—taking photos versus sitting at the front desk of the newspaper and answering the phone.

She arrived at the party early to take pictures of the farm, house, and barn that was still standing. Then, she waited for the news team to arrive, and they all walked in together—the newscaster, the camera man and her. She wasn't sure if she would get to talk to Gunnar but she did. He was still quite sharp, telling her stories about the farm back in the day. An old friend of Gunnar's came over to talk to him, so Rocki moved out of the way to a spot where she could capture some unique shots which she hoped would be worthy enough to make it into the newspaper.

Rocki wished she could've shared the evening with Nick by bringing him along as her guest, but they'd just met and it wouldn't have been right to invite him to meet her work friends until she knew the relationship would last. How she would know that...she had no idea.

Later after the party was done, she'd gone home to set out her clothes for Saturday. The leather jacket, chaps, jeans, shirt, boots, purse, and glasses. She couldn't believe she was actually going to do this. *Ride on a Harley.* She really hoped she liked riding or else it wouldn't end up being a very fun day.

She checked her emails and realized she owed *Mr.Right* a reply to his email.

*Rocki,*

*I am hoping to have some free time this weekend, so I can get a picture taken that looks decent and post it.*

*Do you like James Bond movies?*

*As for the Harley, I usually go riding whenever the weather permits in the late spring, summer and early fall. I'd love to take you riding.*

*Dom*

These darn guys and their Harleys. Well, at least maybe, she could learn all about riding on a bike from Nick. So, when she went riding with Dom, she would know what she was doing.

*Dom,*

*Can't wait to see the picture.*

*I love James Bond movies. In fact, I just plain love watching movies. Saw the new Marvel movie and loved it.*

*Riding on the Harley is always a possibility.*

*Do you read books? If so, what kind? I, of course, love to read Romance novels.*

*Rocki*

Her finger hit send. She really wanted to see his picture so she would feel confident in meeting him. Maybe she would just have to take a chance and meet him without the picture. But then again, maybe not. Enough of *Mr.Right*, she was done thinking about him, she would only think about *Mr.Wrong*. Yes, she needed to concentrate on Nick. A smile spread across her face. Damn, but thinking about him made her feel good. She was done for the night and minutes later, she was in her bed, sleeping and dreaming about Nick.

~

SATURDAY MORNING, Dominick was up early to do his workout. Then he planned to shine up the Harley and put the passenger seat on, along with foot rests on the bike. Thankfully, the weatherman had predicted the day right so far. The skies were clear and the temperatures were rising.

He was ready and waiting when Rocki drove up his driveway. He saw the shock on her face as he watched her through the window. He hoped the size of his house wouldn't be an issue for her. He already knew she liked *him* and that was all he needed.

Damn, but he liked what he saw when she stepped out of her car and walked to his front door.

~

THE NEXT MORNING, Rocki got up, worked out then took a shower. She dressed in the jeans and shirt, then carried the chaps, leather jacket, purse and glasses to the car. She'd already tied her hair back in the leather wrap. The address was programmed into her phone.

Fifteen minutes later, she pulled into Nick's driveway in front of his massive house. She'd thought about doing an aerial view to actually see the house, but hadn't had the time and knew she would see it today, anyway. This had to be one of the largest houses on Prior Lake, if not *the* largest. Wow, she would've never guessed. What an absolutely gorgeous house he had with a four-car garage. One of the garage doors was open and she saw the Harley inside the door, so she pulled behind one of the other doors.

Slowly, she walked up the sidewalk leading to the front door and rang the doorbell.

Only a minute later, Nick opened it to greet her. "Come in, please." He held the door open.

Rocki moved into the foyer. "Nice house." That was all she could manage to say. Even the hallway was magnificent.

"Thanks," he said. "Come in the kitchen for a minute. I'm just finishing my coffee."

Rocki followed him to the kitchen filled with massive windows overlooking the lake. *Wow, he must make a lot of money.* She was way out of her league here. She had a nice house but this was totally different. Hell, it was easily twice the size of her house.

"Would you like a cup of coffee?" he asked.

"No, I'm good." Rocki continued staring out the window at the lake.

Nick finished his coffee quickly. "Follow me."

Rocki followed him out through the garage door. "Let me get my jacket and purse out of my car and lock it."

When she walked back into the garage, Nick was putting on his chaps. Oh wow, he looked so hot while strapping them to his muscled thighs. Rather than gawk at him, she put her chaps on and then her jacket.

Nick started the Harley and easily maneuvered the heavy bike out to the driveway and closed the garage door. "Ready?" he asked.

Rocki had been staring at him, she then caught herself as she nodded her head and got on behind Nick.

"You need to hold on to me when we're riding." He smiled.

"Got it." Rocki felt a bit afraid her nerves were going to get the best of her yet. She put her arms around him and sucked in a breath at the feel of his hard body in her arms.

They were on their way to Mankato.

A couple of hours later, they pulled into Mankato's Main Street downtown now blocked off for the event. They parked and got off then he removed his chaps.

This time, Rocki looked away so she would not be caught ogling him and she took her chaps off, too.

"So, what do you think? I did get you here in one piece, right?"

"I did like it, but I still think it's a bit scary." Rocki smiled.

They put the chaps in the saddle bags then left to walk around to see what was going on. The Lamont Cranston band was playing blues music on the main stage in the street.

"Are you hungry? Let's get some lunch," he suggested.

They walked down the street to a local bar and grill where they ordered burgers and fries. Afterwards, they strolled around the event observing all the bikes, while he explained all the minute details of the different styles of Harleys. He stopped a few times to greet fellow bikers he knew and introduced her.

At around four, they put their chaps back on and headed back to Prior Lake.

At five they pulled into his driveway, Rocki got off and Nick parked the bike in the garage. He took off his chaps.

This time, she did stare. The man was built like a darned brickhouse. Her breath sped up a bit and she gasped out some air. She even felt like it was too hot in the garage or something. She released a soft moan. Getting her thoughts back in place, Rocki finally removed her chaps.

She was far too nervous to look him in the eyes now. So, before she let her hormones have their way, she knew she should probably head home.

"Why don't you come in and clean up a little. We can have a pizza delivered and watch a movie," he said.

Rocki hesitated because she didn't know what to say. She already felt flushed all over from wrapping her arms around that body of his for a whole darn hour. She wanted to go in and hang out with him some more, but she knew she shouldn't because odds were that they would end up in bed.

After all, the image of being in his bed had been on her mind the whole day!

# CHAPTER 27

*"C*ome on, I don't bite," Nick taunted, as he turned and walked toward the house, assuming she would follow.

Rocki stared at his retreating back. She wondered if she could handle it if he even nibbled on her ear. She stifled another nervous groan.

Once he reached the door to the house, he opened the door and turned around. "Coming?" he asked and gave her that wonderful smile of his.

Rocki loved his smile. It alone made her insides melt. So far, he'd been nothing but a gentleman. He hadn't done anything out of line. It had been her who'd had the many multi-faceted impure thoughts all morning. So why was she even hesitating? It was stupid. She was an adult and he was an adult. Well, he'd reduced her to a teenaged girl while undoing those chaps, actually. But worst of all, she wanted to sleep with him and she hoped he wanted to sleep with her. Hell, what was she worried about, probably the worst thing that could happen was that they would have sex. Like great, fabulous send you to the moon sex. So how could that be a bad thing when it was exactly what she wanted? Finally, pulling herself out of the double doubt and dare game she was playing with herself, Rocki bent down to pick up her chaps and purse. Then she smiled up at him and headed to the door where he still stood holding it open.

When she got to the door, Nick kissed her on the forehead. "Thought you would never get here, so I could kiss you." He tipped her chin up with his hand and kissed her lips with a short kiss. He put his arm around her and escorted her inside.

Rocki followed him into the kitchen. The kiss had made her body flush even worse and she wondered if he would think she was crazy if she rubbed an ice cube over her chest. Hiding her nervous smile, she set her purse on the counter then hung her jacket and chaps over a chair.

His eyes were following her every movement. "Would you like a tour of the house?" he asked.

"Thought you'd never ask," Rocki said, although she wasn't sure she could handle anymore splendor than she'd already seen.

He showed her the first floor, and then the second floor where the six bedrooms were located. One bedroom belonged to his daughter who was away at college and one that faced the lake he used for his office because the view was better from the second floor. Each bedroom had its own bathroom. The Master Bedroom was unbelievable, with a deck overlooking the lake, huge whirlpool tub, a shower with zone sensors, along with a massive bed on a pedestal, set up higher than the rest of the room.

Rocki took it all in. All of it matched the man himself. Wide open spaces, all the amenities, wonderful colors, and superior class. Not to mention, it was just as magnificent as he seemed to be.

"If you want to take a shower, you can use one of the guest rooms," he offered. "I'm going to take a shower and change clothes. If you do, there should be everything you need, even a robe."

"I would like that. Which one should I use?" Rocki asked.

"You can use the Red Room," he said.

"Okay, the Red Room it is." Rocki bit at her lip to keep from smiling like an idiot. The red room, the blue room...wow. She sauntered down the hallway to the Red Room and Nick walked into his master bedroom. She closed the door and locked it. It felt so weird to be taking a shower at a strange man's house, but she proceeded to undress then took a shower. The hot water felt wonderful flowing gently over her body. After she finished drying off, she saw a robe hanging on a hook and put it on. She looked in the top drawer of the vanity and found travel size toothpaste, tooth brushes, mouthwash, deodorant, colognes, combs and hair spray. She opened the second drawer and found a hair dryer. She began drying her hair. Luckily, she had some makeup in her purse for touch ups which worked well right now. She put her clothes back on and then finished up with her makeup.

Thirty minutes later, she stepped down the stairs to the main floor.

Nick sat in the Great Room watching the news. He turned the volume down and asked, "Are you hungry? I'm starving."

"I'm hungry, too. What did you have in mind?" Rocki moved further into the room and sat down on the couch across from him.

"Pizza? They deliver," he asked.

"That works for me. I'm not big on veggies. I like sausage and pepperoni."

"We can get it half and half because I'm a big fan of veggies." He got up to get his phone and called in the order. Then he turned back to look at her. "It'll be here in a half an hour. You can get movies on demand from the Smart TV, so let me pull up the list and see what interests you. I have all the streaming services so you can pick a new or old movie." He pulled up the list on the large flat screen television.

"How about the last *Thor* movie? Have you seen it?" Rocki asked and then she grinned at him.

He smiled as he shook his head. "No, have you?"

"Haven't had a chance yet, but I heard it was *good*," Rocki flirted, though she knew she shouldn't.

"*Thor* it is then." Nick chuckled catching on to her teasing. "Let's wait to start it after the pizza arrives."

"Yeah, then we won't be interrupted when all the action is happening." Rocki again teased in a slightly breathless voice. *Come on, Rocki what is the matter with you?* She walked to the patio door to look outside, so she could try to calm her nerves. "You have a great view of the lake from this room, too."

"Actually, almost all the rooms have great views of the lake. I had it built that way." Nick walked up behind her and put his arms around her. "So, what did you think about riding on the Harley? Would you go again?"

Having those strong arms of his around her would not calm her nerves. Not even a little bit. She swallowed heavily then answered, "Yeah, I would go again. I was surprised that all the bikers were so friendly."

"Most are." He turned her around to face him. "Don't think I told you how hot you looked in your leathers. And I'm sure all the guys would agree with me."

"Really?"

"Damn straight. You *are* one hot lady. I'm sure you know that."

This coming from such a hot guy was an overwhelming compliment. "No one's ever said that to me before."

Nick stared into her golden hued hazel eyes. "You're, simply stunning, Rocki." He still had his arms around her.

Before she knew it, his lips were on hers, kissing her deeply. Rocki found herself kissing him back. She was lost, her body felt like it was on fire. He was kissing her with so much passion and intensity, she was sure her body would welcome him in right here and now if he continued. She heard bells ringing and pulled her mouth from his. "Is that the doorbell?"

Nick stopped kissing her but appeared reluctant to end the kissing. "I think that's the pizza." He stared at her lips for a few more seconds then released her and walked to the front door.

And yes, it was the pizza guy.

Nick paid him, took the pizza to the kitchen and set it on the counter.

Rocki couldn't keep her eyes off of him as she walked over to join him and sat on a stool.

Nick took out two plates, napkins, and grabbed two Cokes from the frig. He strode over to sit next to Rocki at the counter, but first he whispered in her ear, "We can finish what we started later. It'll totally be up to you."

Rocki gulped and wasn't sure if she could even trust herself around this man.

They ate pizza and talked about the biker event. When they finished, they moved to the couch, only this time she sat next Nick. He started the movie. The loveseat was a double recliner, so they moved over to sit on it and she grabbed a blanket from a basket by the couch to cover up with since it was a bit chilly in the room.

He put his arm around her, pulling her closer to him.

They watched the movie, both captivated by the film on the large screen with full surround sound. The colors were brilliant on the screen and Thor had a body women would die for. Between watching Thor flex his muscles and showing off his six-pack, and Nick's body pressing against hers with his hand caressing her arm, she thought she might explode right then and there with an orgasm.

Finally, the movie was over. Rocki was relieved yet she wasn't as again, the room was suddenly too warm.

～

DOMINICK TURNED OFF THE TV. He took her hand and led her up to the staircase landing. He studied her face to see if she was with him on this. She looked indecisive, yet her cheeks were flushed, and her eyes looked a bit brighter, more golden, if that was possible. "It's your choice. We won't do anything you don't want to." He hoped she felt the same as he did...because he wanted to do *everything* possible.

Rocki paused and took a deep breath then went up the steps with him to his Master bedroom.

They took off their shoes and laid on his big bed.

Dominick kissed her immediately, captivating her with his deep kisses. He moved downward, kissing her neck and then his hand reached up under her T-shirt to touch her breast.

Rocki sat up and pulled her T-shirt off over her head. The bra of course was still in the way.

This way though, he was able to slip his hand inside it and cup her breast. He moved his hand to her back to unhook the bra. At first, he struggled with the hook, but finally it released and Rocki pulled it off. His hands were all over her breasts and then his mouth devoured the taut dark nipple of one breast. Her body arched in response. He arched up to meet her pelvis. They still had their jeans on, though.

Dominick got up off the bed and stood to take his off and Rocki did the same. Soon, her jeans were lying on the floor. He pulled back the sheets and laid down in the bed.

Rocki still stood there, totally naked except for her thong which she'd left on.

She was so damned beautiful. He couldn't wait to be inside her. He watched her lay down on the bed and immediately, he moved over closer to take her in his arms, rolling her on top of him. His lips met hers, then her neck and finally, her breasts. He maneuvered her to lie on her back and he moved on top of her. He wasn't shy and had already taken off his boxers with his jeans, but he'd pulled the covers up because he didn't want to scare her off in the beginning before they really got started. He'd become rock hard and he wanted to enter her, but he held back and simply pressed against her entrance covered with a sheer piece of material. Now…a wet piece of material.

Trying to take it slow, he kept kissing her and eventually pulled the thong down and off. His hand now found her wet opening and he slid his fingers inside.

Within moments, she reached an orgasm and her body writhed beneath his hand. Rocki then pushed him to his back and was on top of him while kissing him senseless. She kept teasing him mercilessly by rubbing against his hard on.

It had been too long since he'd been inside a woman and even though he didn't want to rush her, he was more than ready. He rolled her over on her back and reached in his nightstand drawer for a condom, he had bought just for tonight. He quickly slid it on. Moving over her again, he kissed her. He delved his tongue in and devoured her mouth with his.

Rocki was panting and gasping as her body continued writhing and arching against his.

"Are you ready?" he asked huskily in her ear.

"Yes," Rocki panted the word out as her hips arched to get closer to his rock-hard erection.

Nick heard her yes and slid inside her slowly till he was completely enclosed by her. She moaned beneath him. Then he moved in and out while picking up speed with each thrust. She moaned again. He was thrusting fast and hard now and he knew he couldn't last much longer.

Rocki cried out with another orgasm.

Finally, he allowed his body to release inside her as he groaned with pleasure, then collapsed alongside her.

"Unbelievable," Nick said.

"Amazing!" Rocki sighed with satisfaction and laid her head on his shoulder.

# CHAPTER 28

*F*eeling more relaxed than she'd felt for a long time, Rocki embraced lying beside Nick, but knew she would eventually have to get up, totally naked and make her way to the bathroom to get dressed and drive home. This would be an extremely awkward situation, one that she hadn't been in since college. Somewhere deep down inside, she knew she could do it.

"I'll be right back." Nick stood up butt naked and strode to the bathroom.

Rocki stared. Yes, she did. The man was definitely well built. Moaning again, she was tempted to get up quickly and get dressed.

Then suddenly, he was back already wearing a robe and handed her one.

"Thanks." She nodded, but while reaching for the robe, the sheet she'd been hanging onto slid down revealing her bare breasts.

Nick's eyes dropped, he couldn't help it. There were bare breasts for his viewing pleasure. He watched her pull the sheet back up. "You know I've already seen them and they are quite lovely. You don't need to cover them up."

"I know." Rocki sat up straight and let go of the sheet. "It's rather foolish to cover up at this point. It's just a bit awkward. We barely know each other."

"I'd like to get to know you much better." Nick stepped over to sit on the side of the bed next to her. He reached over to cup her breast and gazed into her beautiful eyes, a mixture of brown, green and gold. He could clearly see the pleasure his touching was giving her. He kissed her and rolled them over on the bed until she was on top of him and her breasts were within reach of his mouth. "Care to go again?"

"Are you serious?" Rocki asked. She felt him getting hard and erect under her, telling the answer.

"I think you know the answer to that." He pressed his hips upward against her. Next, he rolled her beneath him, shed the robe he had on, and kissed her from the top of her head to her toes as she writhed beneath him. He stopped to put a condom on and pulled her on top of him.

For the next five minutes, Rocki rode him hard screaming out her pleasure while they both climaxed.

After a long while lying quietly in the huge pedestal bed, Nick finally spoke, "It's late. Why don't you stay?"

She was completely exhausted and the idea of getting dressed and driving home seemed like way too much work. "Okay," she groggily answered. Sated beyond her wildest dreams, Rocki fell sweetly to sleep in Nick's arms.

～

WHEN ROCKI WOKE the next morning, she was alone in his bed. Wow. She'd done it. She spent the night at a strange man's house and in his bed. Was she supposed to feel bad? Well, she didn't. It felt good and she felt good.

Nick walked in. "You're up. I'm making breakfast, so why don't you take a shower and come down when you're done. Use my shower."

With that, he was gone. He must've used one of the other bathrooms to shower, as he looked all clean and shiny.

Hesitantly, she stood up to walk to the bathroom, then showered and dressed. The bedazzling scent of bacon cooking drifted up from the kitchen and it smelled delicious. She went downstairs to the kitchen where he'd set the table and was dishing up the food. "Perfect timing," Rocki said.

"I figured about twenty minutes after the shower was turned off." Nick smiled and set a plate in front of her.

Eggs, bacon, toast and hash browns, along with a glass of orange juice already sat on the table. "Very nice," Rocki said. "And it looks good."

"Dig in." He joined her at the table.

"So, you cook, too?" Rocki asked. Though, she already knew how hot he simmered. She kept the goofy smile from showing on her lips.

"I do. And I'm not too bad at it, either."

Her brows rose as she whispered with a sigh in her voice, "Yeah, not too bad, all right."

They both laughed.

They chatted a little about what was on the news and after helping clean up the kitchen, she was ready to go home. "I should get going." Rocki picked up her purse and jacket. "I have things I need to take care of today."

"I'll call you and we'll do something this week."

They walked to the front door where he kissed her and then she left.

～

ROCKI WAS the happiest she'd been in a very long time. She'd just had a night full of unbelievably fantastic sex with a super-hot man who told her she was beautiful. And he said he'd call her. What more could she ask for?

She quickly drove home the few blocks to her house. Who

would've thought they lived so close to each other? After she arrived home, she called Allisa, "How was your date?"

"He was just okay, so I'm going to keep looking," Allisa said. "So, what happened with Nick?"

"I rode with him on the damn Harley to Mankato to the biker event. It was fun. We had a nice time." Rocki couldn't help laughing.

"No, you're not stopping there. Then what happened?" Allisa asked.

"We went back to his house, had pizza and watched a movie."

"And?" Allisa prodded.

"I spent the night, Alli!" Rocki almost squealed with glee.

"Oh, my god! No! You really did it?"

"It was fantastic!" Rocki exclaimed. "Now to see if he wants to go out again."

"If you think it was fantastic, he probably did, too. And if he let you stay the night, he'll call," Allisa assured her.

"You wouldn't believe his house. Seriously, it must be twice the size of mine," Rocki said.

"Well, good for you. You've done good, Girlfriend!" Allisa said.

"Oh, you do not even know. Forget the house. The man is dreamy for sure. Ok...Gotta go. I just got home and have some stuff I need to get done today. Talk to ya later."

Rocki checked her Life Match emails to see if there were any from *Mr.Right*. None from him, but there were responses to her other emails. She actually hadn't expected one from Nick this soon but she didn't want to go out with anyone else right now, even though she wasn't sure Nick was the type to make a commitment. At least not this swiftly. But she still wanted to go out with him and see where it went. Although, she was still curious to meet *Mr.Right*. But only if he sent a picture.

Later in the day, Nick called. "Want to go to the Boat Show downtown on Thursday night?"

"Sounds like fun. Sure," Rocki answered.

"Great. I'll pick you up at six. But I'll need your address," Nick stated.

"Oh, that's right. I'll email it to you," Rocki offered.

"Sounds good. See you Thursday," Nick said.

~

IT WAS Thursday before Rocki even knew it and Nick was picking her up shortly. She'd been cleaning all week, because she wanted it to look perfect when he saw her home.

The doorbell rang and she answered the door. "Come on in." Rocki immediately was pulled into Nick's arms for a kiss. As usual, it was wild, heady, and hot.

Finally, after he had kissed her almost senseless, Nick released her. "Missed you."

"It's good to see you, too." Rocki licked her lips and tried to get herself together. Then she motioned for him to come in. "I'm ready. Just need to make sure everything is off." She went to turn off the lights.

About an hour later, they walked into the Boat Show. Rocki had an older boat and was curious to see what was new with boats.

Nick told her that he was looking for a new boat he could use on Prior Lake and the St. Croix River.

They had a great time looking at all the boats, large and small. Some were downright beautiful. Some were more like yachts.

They made it back to Rocki's house about ten. She showed him around her house that also backed up to the lake. She felt unsure if she should ask him to stay or not.

They were standing in the kitchen by the island counter when he pulled her into his arms and kissed her.

She fell into the kiss like always, drowning herself in the heat of this man.

He kissed her neck and cupped her breast. Then he finally met her forehead with his and softly said, "Love to finish this right now, but it's late and you have to work tomorrow. So, we'll continue this on Saturday. Stevie Nicks is doing a concert at Mystic Lake's new Amphitheater. If you'd like to go, I can get tickets."

"Oh, I love her! I'd love to see her in concert. Sure," Rocki said.

"Saturday it is. I'll pick you up about five, so we can get something to eat first." He gave her a lengthy goodbye kiss. And it was equally as hot as all the others. He gave her that sexy smile of his and said, "We're finishing this Saturday." He left.

Rocki shut the door behind him and felt like she might simply melt and slide down onto the floor into a puddle.

～

ROCKI AND NICK went out twice a week and spent weekends together for the next couple of months. The sex was unbelievably hot every time and they thoroughly enjoyed each other's company. *Mr.Right* continued to email her, but never sent a picture.

Then one Sunday in mid-August, after they'd spent the day on the lake, Rocki heard Nick say what she'd been afraid to even think about the entire time they'd been together. "I think we need to take a little break. We both need to decide where we want this to go. If we both really want this to proceed into a long-term relationship. Besides, I have a writing project I'll be finishing up soon and will be out of town for a few months to put the finishing touches on it."

"You don't want to see me for a few months or never again?" Rocki held back tears threatening to burst free at any minute. She knew it would come down to this, but she hadn't expected it to happen today.

Nick didn't answer.

With her body looking rigid and her fists clenched at her sides, she told him, "Okay, you got it! I'm gone. Don't bother to call me when you get back." Rocki turned away hastily, so he wouldn't see the tears now running down her cheeks, practically ran to her car, got in and left.

# CHAPTER 29

*There* was nothing more Dominick could've said to make the situation easier. What he'd needed was to not see her till the book came out. The longer he deceived her the more he was hurting her and he had to put a stop to it. He felt like crap about all of it, except for the way he felt about her.

Unfortunately, he hadn't realized how much it would hurt to watch Rocki walk away. He figured she would be mad, but he had to do it, so he wouldn't be distracted by her. His thesis needed to be finished by the end of August and the first draft of the book needed to be turned in by mid-September, with the re-writes and editing due by October 15. The book was set to come out the beginning of December. He could only hope she wouldn't forget about him by then and find someone else on Life Match. It probably depended partially on how he wrote the story.

He realized now that he'd fallen in love with her, but this was the first time he'd acknowledged it and now, he wished he'd told her how he felt. Deep down, he felt pretty strongly that Rocki loved him, but after today—all bets were off.

Thanks to Life Match though, he would be able to keep in touch with her secretly by still emailing her as *Mr.Right*. He should've taken it slower and not gotten involved so quickly, but they were made for each other. He knew it. She knew it. But now she was mad as Hell at him, so he really wasn't sure if he had much of a chance to get her back.

Dominick headed inside the house to work on his thesis. The quicker he got the thesis done, the quicker he could get the first draft of the book done. And the quicker he finished the book, the quicker he could contact Rocki again. Then he could come clean and explain what he'd done and why. He could only hope she would listen to him.

Meeting more potential matches for his research had continued, while he gathered more research notes. He'd collected a lot of good information from the dating process and the research info would definitely make a great story.

He knew Rocki hadn't met any more men after the first night they'd had sex. She was a beautiful, sexy, fun, smart, loving, down to earth real person and perfect for him. Why had he let her walk away? The probability of her continuing dating other men on Life Match was high, especially since she'd basically broken off their relationship completely when she told him not to bother calling her in a few months. Hopefully, she didn't mean that.

He walked straight into his office to get started. If she loved him, she would wait for him to call in a few months—December. He was counting on this.

In the meantime, he would send her an email from *Mr.Right*.

*Rocki,*

*Haven't heard from you in a while. Wanted to know if you were still looking for your Life Match.*

*What have you been up to this summer? I've been on the lake boating as often as I can get away from work and as often as the weather cooperates.*

*Hope to hear from you again.*

*Dom*

~

ROCKI HAD CRIED the whole way home. Good thing it was a short drive. She stormed into the house, went straight up to her bedroom, flung herself on the bed, curled up in a ball, and cried. Eventually, she fell asleep.

A couple hours later, she woke with a throbbing headache, got up and took some Tylenol.

Then, she called Allisa who came right over.

"Rocki, I'm so sorry." Allisa put her arm around Rocki.

"I'm so stupid! I knew better! He was the bad boy!" Rocki yelled.

"Yes, you were forewarned. But that doesn't make any difference. He's a bastard for doing this to you." Allisa hugged Rocki. "I tell you what, you just get right back on Life Match and start dating again. Whatever happened to that *Mr.Right* guy?"

"Oh, he emails every once in a while, but he never sent a picture." Rocki started crying again.

"What about the other guys you said were interesting? You can see if they are still interested. It'll be okay, you'll see." Allisa held a sobbing Rocki in her arms and smoothed her hair back from her face.

"Thank God, the kids are gone on internships this summer. Good thing, I never told them about Nick since I wasn't sure if it would last. At least now, I don't have to explain it to them.""It's going to be okay," Allisa soothed. "Go to sleep for a little while. I'll go pick us up some supper and be back."

She laid down on the couch and closed her eyes, willing the Tylenol to work.

An hour later, Allisa was back with a pizza and a pint of Peppermint Bon Bon ice cream—their favorite.

Rocki woke up when she heard Allisa come in. She sat up and wiped a stray leftover tear away. "I'm fine." She walked over to join Allisa at the table.

They ate pizza, watched *Romancing the Stone,* and laughed. Later, they had the ice cream while they watched the news.

"I'm going home. Have to go to work tomorrow, unfortunately. You, however, can call in sick if you need to," Allisa said.

"No. I'm fine. I'll go to work. I'm not going to tell them for a couple of days though. Maybe, I'll do it when I think I won't get all teary eyed. Maybe next week."

"Okay. And tomorrow night you get back on Life Match. You know what they say about falling off the horse, you have to get right back on." Allisa gave her a big hug and left.

Rocki washed her face and got ready for bed.

In bed, she couldn't stop thinking about Nick making love to her. At least, she had thought it was love. It was damn good whatever it was and she refused to feel bad about any minute of her time with Nick. They'd had fun, they'd laughed, and they'd made love— crazy passionate love over and over. One thing she wished was that he would have talked to her about breaking up first. If he had commitment issues, they could've worked on them. Maybe he'd met someone else? Either way, it hurt. But if he could meet someone else, so could she. And she would start tomorrow. After work.

⌒

MONDAY NIGHT AFTER WORK, Rocki was back on Life Match, sending out her mass email to new prospects. She contacted the two guys she'd met before who she'd been interested in. Both were still on and it showed they'd been active recently, so hopefully they'd be interested in meeting again.

*HarleyGuy*, Harvey, had given her his number to call him and said he was interested. She would wait for him to respond to her email and if he did, then she'd call him. She'd been interested in *CaptainJack*, Jack, and he'd sent her an email that she'd never responded to, so who knew if he would still be interested or not. No way to know unless she asked.

She spotted an email from *Mr.Right*. Her heart sped up a little. And it was sent yesterday.

*Rocki,*

*Haven't heard from you in a while. Wanted to know if you were still looking for your Life Match.*

151

*What have you been up to this summer? I've been on the lake boating as often as I can get away from work and as often as the weather cooperates.*

*Hope to hear from you again.*

*Dom*

How perfect that he emailed her yesterday. She responded immediately.

*Dom,*

*How good to hear from you. Were you still interested in meeting?*

*I've been out boating, too. Made it to a few concerts.*

*Did you get the whole picture thing figured out? Can you send me a picture? Maybe you have one on your boat?*

*Rocki*

She hit send.

There were a few new guys that looked interesting. She would see who emailed her back tomorrow and go from there. She felt better today. Maybe after going through the divorce, she'd gotten tougher skinned, which was good in this case, especially. This was definitely time to go by that old saying, *"Out with the old and in with the new."* Because that was exactly what she intended to do. Yes, by the weekend or sooner maybe, she would be meeting new men. And this time she wasn't giving her heart away to anyone. At least, not right away. Maybe after they'd gone out for a year, she would think about it. Yes, that was a great plan and she was sticking to it!

Rocki took a deep breath and whispered aloud, "Nick? Nick who?" Her smile wasn't true but she smiled anyway.

# CHAPTER 30

*R*ocki received at least ten new emails a day from potential matches and set up meetings with the ones who appealed to her.

*HarleyGuy*, Harvey, emailed her and said he'd love to see her again. He set up a date for Friday night at Champs in Eden Prairie for dinner. She accepted.

*CaptainJack*, Jack, emailed her and said he was flying and would be back on Friday and would she like to meet him on Saturday night at Bon Fire in Savage for dinner. Hopefully, if the weather cooperated, they could get a table outside. She accepted.

She received requests to meet and set up times for the next week. *TwinsFan*, Tom wanted to know if she would be interested in attending the Twins game on Sunday afternoon. She hadn't been to the new stadium yet and she liked baseball...so she accepted.

The week flew by and Rocki spent a lot of time trying not to think about Nick. It was Friday and she was meeting Harvey shortly at Champs.

He was waiting outside the front door for her when she walked up. "How have you been?" Harvey asked.

"Good. And yourself?" Rocki asked.

"Busy summer so far," he said as they walked inside to the hostess stand. "Want to sit outside?"

"Sure," she said and they followed the hostess to a table and sat down.

"How has Life Match been working out for you?" Harvey asked.

"Okay."

"Did you meet someone? Is that why you've not been on the site lately?" Harvey asked.

Not much use in lying. Better to get it out in the open. "Yes. Gave it a try, but it wasn't meant to be. Only way you know is to try, right?" Rocki asked.

"Absolutely," Harvey said hopefully.

They ordered dinner and talked about their summers so far.

"I did manage to go riding on a Harley this summer," she stated.

"And did you like it?" Harvey asked as this spiked his interest.

"I guess I kind of got used to it," Rocki said.

"That's great. Would you like to go riding with me? We could take a run down to Stillwater next week on Saturday if the weather is good."

"That sounds like fun," Rocki said.

"Gabby's Bar usually has bands on Saturday night, so we can check it out and do a little dancing, too," Harvey suggested.

They finished eating and walked out to the parking lot. He hadn't ridden the Harley today, instead he had his new Camaro Z28 convertible. She knew he worked with computers but hadn't realized he was well off since he'd only put his income at $75K.

"Nice car," Rocki said as she looked it over.

"Thanks, I really like it," he said as they kept walking to her car, where they stopped. "I can pick you up on Saturday about three. If you want me to pick you up at your house, I need your address."

"Oh, of course," Rocki said and reached in her purse to give him one of her Photography business cards that had her cell number and address.

Harvey took the card and leaned in for a kiss. "If it rains, we'll take the Camaro. See you Saturday." He smiled, then walked back to his car.

Rocki got in her car and drove home. He was a good kisser. There was a spark but nothing like the chemistry she'd felt with Nick. But apparently, you can't always have what you want and she thought Harvey might be the next best thing to that.

~

SATURDAY MORNING, Rocki woke to bright sunshine. It had dawned a picture-perfect day and the water on the lake looked like glass.

Allisa was on her way over.

Rocki was cutting up fruit and setting out croissants for them to eat out on the deck. Their plans were to sit in the lounge chairs by the lake and relax in the sun. She put together a cooler with some ice-cold wine coolers, then set out some chips and dip to snack on.

"You look good." Allisa walked in to see Rocki in her bikini with a sarong tied at her waist.

"Thanks. Got your suit on?" Rocki asked.

"Yup, under my T-shirt and shorts. I'm all set to go." Allisa followed Rocki to the deck where the patio table was set up with their breakfast and sat down. "Wow. Looks good, Rocki."

They both ate and gazed out to the lake. "It's so serene and beautiful. Reminds me of his view...I miss Nick."

"I'm sure you do, but it'll fade with time. Especially, once you get interested in someone new," Allisa said.

"I had a nice time with Harvey last night and he's taking me to Stillwater next Saturday night. Either on his Harley or his new Camaro Z28, if it's raining. The local biker bar in Stillwater has bands on the weekend. So hopefully, we'll be doing some dancing."

"Well, there you go. Off and running already," Allisa said.

"Oh, and he kissed me. He's a good kisser."

"See, it's not all bad," Allisa said.

"Yes, but he's not Nick. Boy, did we have chemistry!" Rocki said.

"Well, yes, but Harvey's interested in going out with you. Nick was too flighty, Sweetie. So, you're moving on," Allisa said.

They finished eating and moved down to the chairs on the beach.

"Tonight, I'm meeting Jack. We'll see how that goes," Rocki said.

"I am happy for you and proud of you, Rocki." Allisa smiled at her.

～

LATER, she met Jack at Bon Fire. The weather held and they were able to get a table outside. Jack was handsome and very charming. He was well-traveled, of course, from being a commercial airline pilot who traveled around the world for his job. But she had heard so many stories about how the pilots slept with all the flight attendants that she wasn't sure he was the type who'd be able to make a commitment to only one woman.

"Rocki, how have you been?" Jack asked warmly after they were seated. "You look great."

"Good. It's been a busy summer so far. How about you?"

"Been doing a lot of flying, of course. I have a classic car, so I go to the old car shows around town. Whenever I have free days, I spend time on my boat on the St. Croix River. Always seems to be something going on in Stillwater in the summer."

"I haven't flown anywhere for a while now. Mainly, I've only been sticking around here, but I certainly wouldn't pass up a chance to travel. I love exploring new places."

"Well, we'll have to see about that. If we end up dating, I'll have to take you away for a weekend. Naturally, I've been all over the world, so I'll let you pick the place."

"Wow, that's a big incentive to go out with you. Good thing you're a nice guy and I kind of like you." Rocki laughed.

He laughed with her. "I'm flying most of the week, next week, but I'm going to a Classic Car show on Sunday. Taking my '55 Chevy. I'd love to have you come along if you're interested."

"Sure, that sounds like fun. I like old cars," Rocki meant it, she liked old cars because they—her ex and her—had a '69 Camaro. He got it in the divorce. Now he and his new girlfriend were probably driving around the city in *her* Camaro. She paused at this thought. It didn't matter anymore, there were more Camaros in the world, and there were more Nicks, -too. Well, maybe not exactly the same ones… but she pushed all those thoughts away.

They sat and talked after dinner for a long time. About life, cars, places he'd seen and places she'd like to see. It was nice. They walked out to her car where he kissed her. A nice kiss. No fireworks were going off or anything like that, but she could work with it. Only a little spark, nothing like Nick, of course. But oh well, she'd see where it went.

On the way home, she couldn't stop thinking about Nick. Damn, this dating thing was supposed to help her forget about Nick, but all it was doing was reminding her of what she was missing. She then again, got mad at herself. Bad boys were losers and he was the one that had lost out.

Sunday turned out to be another picture-perfect day. She met Tom at the Mall of America outside of the Barnes & Noble store. They were taking the Light Rail to downtown Minneapolis for the baseball game.

Tom was about six feet, in shape, with black hair in a short cut and he had cobalt blue eyes.

Very nice-looking man. She liked what she saw. "Hi, I'm Rocki. You must be Tom," she said walking up to him. She knew it was him because he looked exactly like his picture.

"Rocki, good to meet you." He beamed at her.

They made their way down to the Light Rail Transit Terminal and boarded shortly afterwards.

Twenty minutes later, they were downtown and walking to the new Twins Stadium.

Rocki didn't know where their seats were, so she just followed Tom. He made his way to the suites floor and they entered a private suite. Unbelievable, she thought. *Absolutely fabulous seats.* He introduced her to the other people in the suite who were people who worked for Tom at his construction company, Ashton Construction.

Rocki felt a bit shocked because she'd assumed he was a construction worker, *not* the owner of the company.

"Sorry, we're not alone," Tom said. "Mainly, because I was pleasantly surprised when I first saw you at the MOA. You're a very beautiful woman. You never know what to expect with the people you meet on Life Match. Most don't look like their pictures at all, but you certainly do."

"Well thanks. And thank you for making my first experience at the new Twins Stadium so memorable." Rocki smiled at him. *What a sweet guy.*

"No problem. Let's get some food. They just brought in the food trays that come with the suite," Tom said.

Rocki and Tom sat in their box seats, watched the game, and talked about their lives, which tended to be quite similar. They were both divorced and both had been blindsided. The game was action packed with three home runs and the Twins actually won. They took the Light Rail Transit back to the Mall of America.

Tom walked with her to find her car. He gave her a quick kiss. "I'd like to see you again, if you're interested."

The man was even sweet when he kissed. She liked him. "Yes, I'd like that." Rocki reached in her purse and gave him her card, so he could call her.

"Great. I'll call you," Tom gave her a huge smile showing that he genuinely looked forward to seeing her again.

"I have a busy week, but I'm free on Friday night, if that works?"

"Okay, Friday it is. I'll see what's going on in town and give you a call, so we can decide what we'd like to do." Tom strolled away to where his car was parked.

Rocki drove home. How did people pull this off with dating multiple people? She would have to make a decision pretty fast, but how would you know if you didn't first go out with them a few times at least. She had three new people to meet next week and there was no way she would be able to juggle any more men. That's the way it worked though, either she didn't have any men or they all wanted her.

Except, of course, the one she wanted.

# CHAPTER 31

*R*ocki's first date of the week was on Tuesday night where she was meeting *Cassanova*, Santos, at Porter's for a drink after work. Shortly after arriving and taking a seat at the counter, someone gently tapped her shoulder. She turned.

Standing there was a very handsome young man, about twenty years younger than her. He nodded and sat down on the empty stool next to her. "I'm Santos," he said.

"You're kidding, right?" she asked in complete shock.

"No."

"You obviously lied about your age," Rocki said.

"You don't like younger men?" he asked.

"Not when they're the same age as my son!" she exclaimed.

"I have no problem that you are older."

Rocki boldly stared at him. He obviously didn't get it at all. He was way too young for her. On top of that. . .he was a liar. And she wasn't the least bit interested. She stood and walked out.

She was so pissed by the time she got to the car, she started taking deep breaths to calm down. What she really wanted to do was go back in there and slap him across the face. What was he thinking? That she was so desperate she would date a damn kid? Oooh, now she wished she had slapped him! The whole evening had been a waste of time.

Unfortunately, it was simply part of the game. She put the car into drive and drove home.

Wednesday night, she arrived at Apple Bees in Savage to meet *Hunter*, Terry. She stood at the entrance waiting and never saw anyone who looked like Terry's picture.

Ten minutes later, a heavy-set guy, came up to her. "I'm Terry, are you Rocki?" he asked.

Rocki debated on even answering him. She thought about saying no and leaving. That's what she should do. Finally, she answered, "Yes. But I guess I must've read the wrong bio and saw the wrong picture."

"Sorry about that, but if I put down what I actually look like and post a real picture, no one wants to meet me," Terry replied.

She was pissed. "But you have to realize that it's wrong to fool someone like this."

"I have to though, people are so…" He shook his head. "Want to get a table?"

"No, thanks. I refuse to date anyone who isn't honest." Rocki turned away from him and walked out the door hoping to Hell, he didn't follow her out. She walked directly and at a swift pace to her car, got in and locked the door. Only then did she dare to look back to see if he'd followed her. Thank God, he hadn't. She started the car and drove home.

She couldn't believe it. Why was she having such bad luck with the matches now? Thank heavens, she had three good ones to go out with or this could be quite depressing.

Thursday night, she met *MovieMan*, Mel, at Chili's in Burnsville. She walked in and recognized him sitting at the counter right away. She walked over and sat down next to him. "Hi, I'm Rocki, you must be Mel."

"Yes, good to meet you," he said.

He smelled gross, but she couldn't figure out what it was exactly. This wasn't good. In fact, he was just plain creepy. He at least could've put on some cologne for a date! This was a bad sign as to his hygiene and personality. After the fiascos of the last two nights, she simply wanted to leave, but that would've been extremely awkward.

The bartender came over and they ordered drinks.

"What is with the *MovieMan* name?" she asked trying to make conversation and thinking maybe they could talk about movies for a little bit and then she could leave.

"All I do is watch movies. Mainly, Porn. Do you like Porn?" he asked.

"Not really," she answered. "I need to use the restroom." Rocki got up and went in the restroom. She stood there for a few minutes, then walked to the entrance door and straight out to her car where she immediately locked the door. She turned quickly to see if smelly porn man had followed her. The coast was clear, so she immediately started the car and left.

Hell, she couldn't even call Allisa about this nightmare date because she was out on a date.

Once home she made herself something to eat and sat down on the couch to watch TV. *Wow, tonight really sucked.* The rest of the weekend would be better she told herself. At least Harvey, Jack and Tom were what she would call *normal* guys. At least she thought they were.

Tom called a little later, which lifted her spirits immensely. He wanted to know if she'd be interested in going to the Cold Play concert. She said she'd love to.

On Friday, she immediately changed clothes after getting home. She put on her tight skinny leg blue jeans, a long flimsy top, and her four-inch sandals.

He arrived promptly at six to pick her up. He had a new Corvette convertible but the top was up.

Rocki had been waiting by the window, so she immediately, locked the door and went out to meet him.

The tickets for the concert were front row in the first risers on the side of the stage, which proved to be excellent seats. The show was fabulous and they went for a burger afterwards at Burger Joe's. They talked about their lives and enjoyed each other's company. Tom dropped her off at her house and she debated on inviting him in. It was late though, so she didn't.

He walked her to the door. "I'd like to see you again," Tom said.

"Me, too," she said.

Tom pulled her towards him and kissed her.

It was a nice sweet kiss. Just like the man who gave it to her. Didn't rock her world or anything, but it wasn't bad either.

"I'll call you and we can do something next week." He smiled at her as he gave her a nod of his head.

"I look forward to it." Rocki opened the front door. She walked inside, then watched him leave from the window beside the door, which was now closed.

Saturday, Harvey picked her up about three. She dressed in her leathers and was ready to go when he arrived. The weather was excellent, sunny and clear skies, when they left. She got on the bike behind him and they were on their way to Stillwater.

Once there, they took off the chaps and jackets then placed them in the saddle bags. She'd worn her black leather halter top, since the temperature would reach the eighties. They strolled down Main Street looking in windows and had dinner on the Freight House's deck overlooking the river. Later, they strolled down the sidewalk along the river to watch the boats and people.

When the sun was setting, they rode the bike over to Gabby's Bar and parked it in the parking lot along with a multitude of bikes. They strolled inside to listen to the band playing oldie songs that were made for dancing. Harvey held her tight during the slow dances, pressing her body against his. When the song ended, he kissed her. She wanted him to kiss her more. The kisses weren't like Nicks, but there was something there. Rocki realized that she really felt something at last!

About midnight, he dropped her off at her house. At the door, he kissed her with a kiss that promised more.

She could tell he sensed she didn't feel comfortable inviting him in yet, though and ended the kiss.

He gave her a winning smile. "I'll call you. We can do something next week." He walked over to the bike and left.

Rocki went inside. Hell, she had no idea what she was doing. It was a lot simpler with Nick. She just knew it felt right from the very beginning. But then suddenly out of nowhere...it hadn't been right for him anymore.

〜

SUNDAY AT NOON, Jack picked her up in his '55 Chevy and they went to a Classic Car show at the Dakota Fair Grounds. She loved his car. But you couldn't date a guy simply because you liked his car, she wasn't 18 anymore. She admonished herself. A part of her wished she still owned her old Camaro. They strolled around and looked at cars while holding hands. Every so often, they would stop to talk to guys Jack knew.

Afterwards, they went to Katy's Diner for dinner.

Jack was a great guy. She enjoyed his company. They talked about their likes and dislikes, ultimately showing they had a lot of things in common.

At about eight, he brought her home and walked her to the door. "I'd like to see you again," he said holding her hand.

"Definitely, a good idea," Rocki said laughing.

Jack smiled, took her in his arms, and kissed her.

She liked Jack so much, but she wished the chemistry was stronger. She was willing to give it some time though.

Jack left and Rocki went inside. The more she thought about the whole chemistry thing, the more she came to the conclusion that maybe it was just her and she wasn't being completely open to having feelings for someone else because she still had feelings for Nick. Well, that was just great. She would have to make those feelings go away, because he wasn't coming back.

In fact, he'd never even called her again, after that day.

And of course, to mess with her head a little more, she received an email from *Mr.Right*, Dom, with a picture.

163

## CHAPTER 32

*D*ominick printed out a final copy of his Master's Thesis. He'd spent way too many grueling months collecting all the information and putting it all together, but he'd done it. And he was pleased with the final paper. The thesis was a research paper though and the book would be something totally different. This story would be written from a guy's point view and would basically be about his journey to find a woman who would be a perfect match, using the internet dating sites.

To make it more real, he used bits and pieces from his internet dating experiences.

It was a beautiful, sunny, hot day on the last day of August and he decided to treat himself to a leisurely drive in his Corvette, with the top down, on the way to Hamline University in St. Paul. He'd been working way too hard for the past month and hadn't taken any time off for fun. He'd been on a deadline schedule to get the thesis done, but now he would be moving forward on the book. Finishing the book was a priority, because the sooner it was done, the sooner he could patch things up with Rocki. That was if she was still speaking to him at all by then. He pulled up and parked.

Hamline was an old, old school with large buildings from the

1880's era. Well-built and still magnificent structures. The grounds were impeccably landscaped, including gardens and fountains. Actually, it created a very serene and relaxing atmosphere. He walked into Sutter Hall, which housed the Fine Arts classrooms and professor's offices where he found Professor Drewberry's office.

"Dominick, good to see you man," Professor Drewberry said. "Come on in."

Dominick smiled at him. "It's done. Finally. Took longer than I expected, but it's good."

"Well, if you're pleased with the results, I'm sure I will be, too."

"I hope so. I'll be finishing the first draft of the manuscript soon. Hope to have it to my editor by mid-September or sooner."

"I imagine you will be changing it up quite a bit in the book." Professor Drewberry flipped quickly over the edges of the printed pages of the thesis. "I'll start reading this tonight. I'll email you when I'm done and let you know if I have any suggestions for the book."

"Okay. That sounds good. I'm going to get going, so I can enjoy my one day of freedom." Dominick left the building and strolled slowly back to where he'd parked the Corvette. The urge to call Rocki had gotten to be overwhelming. He wanted to share his accomplishment with her, but even if he could call her, he wasn't sure she would think it was an accomplishment at all at this point. But damn, he just wanted to hear her voice. Hell, he wanted way more than that. He wanted her sharing his bed again. But he knew that wasn't going to happen, so he got in the car and drove to Matt's Bar to pick up a burger basket to bring home. He was treating himself to a movie tonight on his big screen TV. Surely, there was a newly released movie on demand he hadn't seen yet. Then in the morning, he would start working on the final pages of the manuscript. Hopefully, it would go swiftly.

~

ON THE LAST day of August, he typed in the final pages of the manuscript. It had turned out damn good, if he didn't say so himself!

He liked the story's end and hoped his and Rocki's ending would turn out just as good. The book was really Nick and Rocki's story anyway, containing bits and pieces of their dating journey with each other plus other matches he'd met along the way. It would be interesting to see how their real story ended. He was used to writing endings the way he wanted them to end, so he intended to give it his best try with their real-life story.

He couldn't believe how badly he wanted to call Rocki. Then again, he thought about her a lot. Dreamed of her many nights and had wanted to feel her in his arms again, more times than he cared to admit. He'd felt like a piece of him was missing and he knew the woman was meant to be with him.

He hoped he still had a chance with her.

The goal line and his prize were in sight.

Dominick finished his edits the next day and sent his email to Sandy, his editor, along with the attached word doc, containing the whole book.

He planned on meeting a friend at Mystic Lake Casino for their fabulous buffet then play a little Black Jack, as his treat for finishing the book.

After his night out, he couldn't help himself and sent Rocki and email from *Mr.Right*. He'd sent her an email last week, just so she wouldn't forget about him and because he needed that little bit of contact with her. This was the big day for both of them and he was sending her a picture. The first one. She'd kept asking and now, she would finally get one.

He'd had a friend take a picture of him on a boat—not his because she would recognize it—but instead on his friend, Dan's boat. He wore a baseball hat, sunglasses and he'd let his beard grow while he was on his writing marathon. They took the picture at dusk, so the picture was dark and she wouldn't be able to recognize him. He'd been waiting to send it. Waiting for a special occasion and this was it. He'd finished the damn book!

*Rocki,*

*I've been busy with work projects, but wanted to take the time to send you*

*the picture you've been waiting for, so that you can finally meet me in person*
*on a real live date. Hope you've been able to get out and enjoy the great*
*weather we've been having lately.*

*Can't wait to meet you.*

*Dom*

Dominick hit send and eagerly anticipated her reply.

Tomorrow, he would be taking Ryder to the great Minnesota State
Fair for a day of sampling old and new food delights on a stick and
not on a stick. It was a tradition for their family to go visit the Fair
every year and still to this day, he looked forward to attending. He
was glad Ryder still even wanted to go with him, but she said she
wouldn't miss it for the world. She would go a second time with
friends, of course. It was the Labor Day weekend, and he would also
be spending some time on the lake with Ryder and her friends.


HOPEFULLY, Sandy would have some proofs back to him by Tuesday.
She was a workaholic and once she started reading, probably wouldn't
be able to put it down. At least, he hoped she wouldn't be able to put it
down, because that would mean he'd done a great job writing.

Tuesday came too soon. Ryder left to go back to Gustavus and
Sandy had already sent back one hundred pages with edits. He made
the changes and sent them back to her by the end of the week right
before she sent the next one hundred pages. He was pumped! At this
rate, he could complete the edits by the third week of September.
Then he would do one more read through to check for any errors like
missing or misspelled words. At that point, it would be ready to
publish.

Promptly on the morning of the first day of October, he received
an email from Sandy stating she'd signed off and sent it to the print
department. He would receive a cover proof by the next week to ask
for changes or approve. They were ahead of schedule and would be
shooting for a release date of November twentieth which would put it
out in plenty of time for Thanksgiving. The publicity department
would be getting back to her on the dates set up for book signings.

She wanted to do a big one the weekend after Thanksgiving at the Barnes & Noble in the Mall of America. After all, he was a New York Times Bestseller Author.

*Almost there*. Soon, he could call Rocki.

He'd sent her an email each week as *Mr.Right*. She'd replied that the picture wasn't very clear but was glad he'd sent one. After he'd received the email from Sandy stating the book was set to release in both print and digital mid-November as planned, he sent Rocki an email asking her to meet him as *Mr.Right* for dinner at Porter's Steakhouse in Lakeville on Saturday night.

She accepted.

With the book completed, he could move on with his life and he definitely wanted Rocki in his life. He really hoped she would want the same thing.

On Saturday, Dominick dressed to meet Rocki. He decided to leave the beard although he cut it close to the skin so it looked more like a five o'clock shadow than a beard. He then put on his darkest sunglasses and borrowed Ryder's Chevy Tahoe. He couldn't show up in Nick's Escalade, right?

$\sim$

ROCKI SPENT the next weeks dating Tom, Jack and Harvey while trying to find even a fraction of the passion she'd felt for Nick, before she would take the next step and sleep with one of them. She knew she needed to go through the process of elimination and get down to one, soon.

Jack became the front runner, next Harvey and then Tom.

Jack asked her to pick a place she wanted to go to for a weekend and he would plan it out. Maybe she needed to just go for it and see what happened?

She couldn't believe *Mr.Right*, Dom, kept emailing her. If he really wanted to meet her, he simply needed to send a picture. Then when he finally did, it was so dark that it was extremely hard to even see his features, but he looked passable anyway. She would give it a shot. What did she have to lose?

She'd pretty much blown it with her other men, anyway.

Tom quit calling first. Unfortunately, after almost two months, it became apparent guys expected a woman to be willing to sleep with them. If she didn't feel the same, they weren't wasting anymore time. And Tom had moved on. She hadn't felt an uncontrollable desire to sleep with him. And if it wasn't there by then, it probably wouldn't be there in the future, either.

Harvey was the one she'd felt some passion for, but his lifestyle didn't fit hers, so she simply couldn't see the point. He was so into riding the Harley, it didn't leave room for much else. She'd felt like he was running away from something he'd never dealt with. Regardless, it wasn't her style. Too bad, he was such a hunk and great kisser. When he gave her the ultimatum of deciding if she was going to sleep with him or not, she had to be honest and tell him it just wasn't going to happen. Even though a part of her had wanted it to work, she knew deep down it wouldn't, so it was best to walk away.

With Jack, it had always been fun and she had so wanted it to work out, but the desire simply wasn't there. Only a couple of weeks ago, she'd flown to Palm Springs with him for the weekend. He'd been charming and was a perfect gentleman. She'd made it as far as taking off her clothes and getting in bed with him with every intention of having sex. When it became apparent to both of them that she wasn't turned on the way she should've been, they merely went to sleep after he took a quick shower to take care of what she hadn't.

He was pleasant the next day on the flight home, but hadn't called again.

Rocki couldn't blame him one bit.

So, when she received the invitation from Dom, she was game to give it a shot. And tonight, was the night. She put on a short body-hugging black dress and spiked black heels.

*What the Hell! Never know what might happen.*

# CHAPTER 33

*R*ocki pulled up at Porter's Steakhouse, parked, and walked to the door. She'd lucked out on the weather, it was the third week of October, typically MEA—Minnesota Educators Academy—teacher's conference, a no school week for most kids, and Minnesota was having as they like to call it, Indian Summer with temperatures in the high seventies. With the warm temps, she didn't need a jacket, which worked well to show off her still tan legs and arms.

Outside the door, a man was waiting and her heart skipped a beat. He was definitely hot. He had a close-cropped beard, almost looked like a two-day shadow, and designer sun glasses. The short-sleeved tan button down shirt was open at the neck showing off a sliver of his tan chest. He wore black dress pants with expensive Italian black dress shoes. His thick blond hair was cut short and he had an intoxicating smile that drew her in.

As she walked closer to him, he walked towards her closing the gap until he was directly in front of her.

"Rocki?" he asked.

"Yes," she answered.

"Dominick," he said.

"Nice to finally meet you," she said wondering if maybe her luck had finally changed, although there was something familiar about him.

He put his hand around her back to guide her inside. She felt warmth spread through her body at his touch. *What is going on? This simply cannot be happening.*

The hostess showed them to a table and they sat down. The lighting was dim but he didn't remove his sunglasses. After the hostess handed them menus and left, the waitress brought a bottle of wine and poured a little in his glass. He tasted the wine then nodded. The waitress filled both their glasses and disappeared.

Rocki wished the lighting was better, so she could see him and she wondered why he hadn't taken off his sunglasses yet.

"It's been a while," he said.

"What?" she asked.

"I've been looking forward to seeing you," he whispered as he sent a wicked smile her way.

"I've wanted to meet you for a long time," Rocki said, as she stared at him, wondering why his voice sounded so damn familiar.

◞◟

DOMINICK WATCHED Rocki from behind his sun glasses for any sign of recognition on her part. He was trying to say as little as he could so she wouldn't recognize his voice. He was actually regretting meeting her tonight as the reality of the situation hit him. He needed to be prepared if she freaked out on him. She had every right to be pissed off when she realized who he was.

Best to get it over with he decided, though. He set the glasses on the table and watched for her reaction.

"Rocki," he said.

She didn't say anything, simply froze in place.

He then spoke again, "It's me."

"Oh, my God!" she exclaimed. "I don't believe it! How could you?" she asked.

171

"Rocki—" he started.

Rocki's cell phone rang.

Dominick waited as she answered it. After all, he had waited all this time, he could wait another few minutes. Anything to get a chance to explain this to her.

～

DAMN IT SHE forgot to turn it on vibrate. Rocki pulled it out of her purse and saw it was Allisa. It was odd that she would call now when she knew she was meeting Dom. *Very odd.* She tapped the phone to answer the call. "This is not a good time—."

Allisa cut her off. "Rocki, pick up your purse and walk outside to talk to me. It's important!"

Rocki did as she said, picking up her purse and walking outside. "What is it?" she asked Allisa over the phone.

"Go to your car. You need to sit down," Allisa said.

"Okay, I'm almost to the car," Rocki said. Minutes later, she was inside her car. "Okay, I'm sitting. What is it? What else could possibly go wrong tonight?"

"Nick is Dominick Taggart, a big New York Times Best Seller author, and—."

"I don't care who he is!" Rocki shouted into the phone.

"His new book, *Match Made in Heaven*, is being released November twentieth," Allisa said.

"So? Why do I care?" Rocki asked.

"The book is about internet dating," Allisa said.

"Oh, my God! And you think he wrote it about me?" Rocki asked. She started the car and backed out of the parking spot. She glanced at the door and saw Dom, Nick, Dominick or whoever the Hell he was, standing at the door watching her leave.

"Rocki, I'll meet you at your house. Okay?" Allisa said.

"Okay," Rocki said as tears temporarily blinded her eyes as she frantically swiped them away.

Minutes later, she drove up her driveway with Allisa right behind her. Rocki pulled in the garage and stepped out of the car.

Allisa parked then ran to Rocki and embraced her. "Oh, Rocki, I'm so sorry. I wanted you to know as soon as I found out. He's a bastard to do that to you," she said as they walked in the house, closing the garage door on their way.

They sat down in the Great Room on the couch.

Rocki was sobbing at this point. "I was stupid and fell in love with him! Probably both of them, Nick and Dom."

"It happens to the best of us. I'll be willing to bet by the time you finish reading his book, you won't be in love with him anymore," Allisa said, reaching over to get her oversized purse. She took out a softcover book and handed it to Rocki.

"What's this? I thought you said it wasn't released yet?" Rocki asked.

"It's called an ARC which stands for Advanced Reader Copy," Allisa explained. "The book stores get them ahead of time, so they can read the book before it comes out. That way, hopefully, if they like it, they'll have good things to say about it when it's released."

"How'd you get it? Did you read it?" Rocki asked.

"A friend of mine works at Barnes & Noble. The ARC just came in and when she read the back to see what the book was about and saw it was about internet dating, she thought of me. She knew I'd been trying internet dating and asked if I wanted to read it. All I have to do is post a review after I'm done." Allisa handed the book to Rocki.

"So did you read it?" Rocki asked.

"Just picked it up after work, so I only had time to read the first chapter. Do you want me to read it first? Or do you want to?" Allisa asked.

"I'd like to..." Rocki looked at the book and checked the back cover flap to see if he had a picture. Sure enough. It was Nick. Or Dom. Or Dominick, whatever his real name was.

"I take it you read the Bio? Of course, that's why you called, because you knew Dom and Nick were the same person. Which means *Mr.Right* and *Mr.Wrong* are one and the same, which is the conclusion I'd just came to after meeting Dom at Porter's Steakhouse," Rocki said as she rambled on.

"Yes. When I saw the picture, I knew he was Nick. Not sure about Dom," Allisa said.

Rocki closed the book and held it to her chest. "I'll be fine. Don't worry about me. I'm going to get ready for bed and climb in to do a little reading."

"Good. Don't do anything crazy though. Promise?" Allisa asked.

"Promise," Rocki said, as she opened the door for Allisa to leave.

Shortly afterward, Rocki crawled into bed with the book. After reading the first chapter, she was absolutely sure it was about her and Nick. She couldn't continue. The story was too close to her heart and she knew it would probably take time to read the whole thing. She closed the book and opened it to the back flap, so she could see Nick's picture.

*Why hadn't she caught on to his little charade sooner?* Like when he finally sent the picture. Plus, she should've known it was him as soon as he opened his mouth at Porter's. *Had he left shortly after her sudden exit?* Mainly, she wondered what he was thinking about now. Maybe, she should've gone back in and let him explain. But what was there to explain? It was plain and simple. He'd lied to her! And what had she always said and believed?

You simply cannot have a relationship based on one lie after another.

# CHAPTER 34

*D*ominick paid the check and went home. He'd blown it royally. She was mad as Hell and she had every right to walk out on him. Now, he needed to give her a chance to cool down.

He didn't even care to admit how many times he'd picked up the phone to call her after that night, only to set it back down without making the call.

The next weeks, he spent getting ready for the marketing aspect of publicizing his new book release.

Dominick planned his book tour right up to Christmas. He would be traveling virtually the whole month. Not his idea of a fun time but he would do what he needed to do to sell books. Not a day went by when he didn't think about Rocki and every inch of his body wanted to call her, but he knew he needed to give her some space. Hell, she'd basically walked out on him and left him sitting at the table. It was her call. What he'd done wasn't right, and he knew it. But he just needed the chance to at least explain what he'd done and why. And most importantly, he wanted a chance to apologize and tell her how he felt. How he'd fallen for her. Now, he may never get the chance.

ROCKI SPENT the next weeks reading, *Match Made in Heaven*, one chapter a day. That was all she could manage to get through each day, because by the time she got to the end of a chapter, she was crying. The whole damn story was about her and Nick. She wasn't even sure she wanted to read the end, but she was curious to see how he wrote the end of the story.

However, there was one thing she wanted to know— how their real-life story ended.

*Or had it already?*

So even though it made her cry, she kept going and was getting closer to the end. Now even more she didn't want to read the end because she felt once she got to that point, it would be the end of her and Nick. *What did that say about her? Was she still in love with him?*

After a while, Rocki had calmed down a lot and she tried to understand why he'd done it. She'd felt sure he had feelings for her. Their chemistry was so damn good! But in the end maybe he realized their internet dating story was exactly what he needed for the book and it would totally look like he used her. So, it was best to dump her and deal with the fallout later.

She knew him as a kind warm man and she couldn't believe he had set out to hurt her. At times, she thought that she really should give him a chance to explain. If he ever called her again, she would at least give him a chance to explain.

She picked up the book and read another chapter before going to sleep. In the morning, she went outside to pick up the Sunday paper lying on the driveway and read it while she ate some breakfast. *Unbelievable!* On the front page of the Variety section was Nick's face. He was featured in the book section with a large picture of him holding his book. She gasped, but started reading anyway. He was having a book signing at the Mall of America next Saturday. Well, she certainly wasn't going to go to it. But then again, it would be a chance to see him and if a lot of people showed up for the signing, he wouldn't even notice her.

The week went by and on Friday night, she read the last chapter. She was in tears again, but this time it was because she was happy.

He'd given the Hero and Heroine a happy ending. He'd written how he felt about the heroine...her obviously. He loved her and there had not been a day since he'd met her that he didn't think about her. He'd hated lying to her and so he asked her to wait and see if they were moving too fast. Then he intended to go to her after the book was done and try to win her back. She was the love of his life, at least that was what he'd written—his perfect match.

His Ms. Right!

He was a damn good writer, she'd give him that.

In the morning, she got up early and called Allisa. "I need you to go to the Mall of America with me today. Can you be here in an hour?" Rocki asked.

"You're serious? This is pretty short notice, don't you think?" Allisa asked.

"Nick is doing a book signing at the Mall of America at one o'clock. I need you to go with me, so I don't do anything stupid."

"Okay. I'm getting dressed as we speak. I'll be at your house at eleven so we can get there early," Allisa said.

Rocki put on a pair of her designer jeans, a sweater wrap, and her new kick ass brown leather boots. She was ready but she needed to do one more thing. She went in her office, took out a piece of fancy colored stationary and sat down at her desk.

She wrote six simple words:

*So, how does our story end?*

And signed it, *Rocki*. She folded it, put it in an envelope, and slid it in her purse, moments before Allisa arrived. She walked out, locking the door behind her, then got into Allisa's car.

A long line had already formed when they arrived, so Rocki was glad they'd arrived early. They walked around to the end of the line. When they got closer, they each purchased a book for Nick to autograph.

Nick was busy looking down to sign books and didn't seem to notice them until they were right up to the table, directly in front of him. "Rocki," Nick said.

The people around them gasped.

"Nick," Rocki said, not sure why everyone was looking at her. She hadn't even done anything. Yet. She handed Nick the book to sign. He picked it up and she watched him write her name along with something else then sign his name. She pulled the envelope out of her purse and handed it to him.

Nick opened the envelope and read her note.

*So, how does our story end?*

*Rocki*

The crowd was getting restless so Allisa handed him her book to sign.

Looking stunned, he seemed to be at a loss for words. Then he finally spoke, "We need to talk. I'm on tour and won't be back until Christmas. I really want to see you and talk to you. I hope you will give me that chance. Dinner at seven on Christmas Eve at my house?" Nick asked.

Rocki picked up her book. "Okay. Christmas Eve it is." She turned and walked off the signing table platform.

Allisa followed her. "Well done," she said as they walked out of the mall.

"I thought it went very well," Rocki said. "Now, all I can do is hope the days fly by until Christmas Eve.

~

DOMINICK WATCHED them leave as another book was placed in front of him. Hot damn! He wanted nothing better than to write a happy ending to his and Rocki's story.

"Was that the Rocki you dedicated the book to?" the man who handed him the book asked.

"Yes."

"Good luck."

"Thanks. I'm probably going to need it!" Dominick continued signing books for the next hour, only now he was smiling because all he could think of was winning Rocki back.

# EPILOGUE

Christmas Eve

*R*ocki hadn't heard a word from Nick since the book signing at the Mall of America, but she felt confident about seeing him tonight. She'd missed him so much she could hardly stand it. At night, she'd dreamt about Nick making love to her all night long and waking up in his arms. Then in the morning, she chided herself. She shouldn't just fall into bed with him immediately. Though she knew she wanted to be with him.

Despite the lecture she kept giving herself, she went on with getting ready for her meeting with the hottest man she'd ever been with. A man who could kiss her until she didn't even know her own name. Ignoring the self-scolding, Rocki put on her new Victoria Secret red sexy push-up bra and matching skimpy thong. She pulled on her little red skin-tight dress that hugged her body, showing off her legs in matching red heels. She curled her hair, then gave her makeup a once over.

Rocki wanted Nick and she also wanted him to see what he'd been missing. She wasn't sure if they would have sex just yet…however, she did want for him to want her badly. Then maybe she would make him wait a while.

Of course, she hadn't appreciated how he'd fooled her with his whole internet dating experiment, but in the end, they'd both fallen in love and she was going to forgive him. But he did need to ask her to forgive him first.

And he'd better as this was the one thing she needed before they could have anything together.

~

DOMINICK HAD ARRIVED home only a few days ago. He decorated the house with his daughter, Ryder, who was home from college and was ready for his big night with Rocki. Ryder was meeting some friends and wouldn't be home until later in the evening.

Ryder kissed him goodbye on the cheek and was off to catch up with her friends at Champs.

He closed the door behind her. The Christmas lights were on and cast a golden hue to the Family Room. The rest of the lights were turned down low. A bottle of wine chilled on the counter beside a small wrapped present with a gold bow.

Dominick hoped that this Christmas, he would have the woman who was the perfect match for him in his arms.

~

ROCKI PULLED into Nick's driveway, parked the car, and gazed out the window at his house, glowing with Christmas lights lining practically every inch of the house. She walked up to the door, feeling very apprehensive, as her nerves almost got the best of her. She thought about going back to the car instead of going forward to the door, but she didn't. This was a big night for her. There always was the chance the night wouldn't go the way she wanted it to, but she couldn't wait to see his face and she desperately wanted to kiss him. At least one more time!

She rang the doorbell.

A few minutes later, the door opened and Nick was standing in front of her. "Rocki."

"Nick, it's so good to see you." Rocki walked into his house.

He motioned for her to go into the Family Room.

She paused by the bar counter where he began opening a bottle of wine and poured them each a glass. He handed her one and she sat down on a bar stool. She took a sip to bolster her nerves.

"I just returned home from the book tour a couple days ago. It was grueling, but it appears the book is a hit." He sat down on the bar stool next to her.

"Our book you mean?" she asked.

"Yes, *our* book. I wanted to explain the book to you in person."

"Now's your chance." She waited for his explanation. Rocki did not intend to make this easy for him. What he did had turned her world upside down. She needed to hear this from him.

"I set out to do my thesis on internet dating and to do that required research on the subject. The only way to do that was to give it a try. I wanted to see how the whole process worked. Most people think there are a lot of guys out there who are only looking for women to have sex with. The so-called *bad boys*. Unfortunately, for the women, they are looking for the good guys who will make a commitment. So my research was to see how many of the same women would go out with *Mr.Right* and *Mr.Wrong*."

"I kept saying no, but you were persistent and I wanted to see what you looked like in person." Rocki tried to justify her actions.

"I know. I'm sorry I kept after you to go out with me. But after I saw you at the Cheese Cake Factory, I knew I had to meet you."

"That was you at the Cheese Cake Factory?" she asked with a gasp.

"Yes. I think I fell in love with you that day. I already knew all about you from your Life Match file and knew we would be a good match. But when I saw you in person and knew you looked as good as your picture, I was hooked."

Rocki laughed. "Really."

He nodded his head. "That's why I was so insistent you go out with me." Nick finally smiled. "So why did you agree to go out with me as *Mr.Wrong?*"

"I hoped I wouldn't like you, so I simply wanted to meet you and get it over with."

"But instead, you liked me?"

"Yes. Unfortunately."

Nick tilted his head back a little at this answer. "So why did you agree to sleep with me?" He smiled wickedly and reached out to hold her hand.

"Because the chemistry we had was unbelievable. Plus, I'd always done everything by the book and it had gotten me absolutely nowhere, so I thought what the heck? Might as well have a little fun. Somewhere I'd heard the song lyric, 'How about spending some time with Mr. Wrong while you're looking for Mr. Right'. It sounded like the thing to do at the time."

"I'm glad you did. Rocki, I fell in love with you almost immediately. Unfortunately, I felt like the longer I went on with that *Mr.Wrong* persona, the more I was hurting you. So, I put a stop to it. I couldn't go on deceiving you like that. I wanted to tell you then, but I had to finish my research and get my thesis paper turned in."

"How did research for a thesis turn into a book about us?" she asked.

"I'm a writer, Rocki. It's what I do. Our story was great, so I wrote it. I knew it would be a best seller."

"At my expense, though?" Rocki held onto his hand and searched his enchanting blue eyes for the love he'd just confessed. She saw it and knew she'd found her Mr. Right.

"I'm so sorry. I never meant to hurt you. I love you, Rocki."

"I was deeply hurt when you abruptly ended our relationship with no explanation."

"I was going to tell you that night at Porter's but you left when you realized I was both *Mr.Right* and *Mr.Wrong*. You didn't give me a chance to explain anything. I figured you hated me and didn't want anything else to do with me."

"Of course, I was mad. You lied to me. I loved you and you played me for a fool."

"You love me?" he asked.

Rocki nodded. "So, what happens now?"

"I want you to know I'm giving you a portion of the proceeds from the book. I could never have done it without you." Nick reached behind the counter for an envelope with her name on it containing a check for her portion of the royalties and laid it on the counter in front of her. Then he handed her a small wrapped present. "Open it."

"I didn't bring you anything." She stared at the present in her hands.

"Just you showing up here is the only gift I wanted. Go ahead and open it."

Rocki ripped the wrapping paper off the small box and removed the lid. Inside was a diamond ring sparkling up at her. First shock, then joy crossed her face.

Nick got down on his knee in front of her. "Rocki, I hope you can forgive me. I am madly in love with you and want to spend the rest of my life with you. Making love to you and living life to its fullest with you. Will you do me the honor of marrying me?"

Rocki couldn't believe what was happening. Nick had made her happier than she had been for over three years and he'd said the words she needed to hear. Simply looking at him, she saw the first man in years who'd even sparked any interest in her. He was every-thing she'd ever dreamed of and never thought to find in any man.

"Yes."

Nick released a nervous breath as he'd been watching her face the entire time as it flashed between shock, surprise and sheer joy. He stood up as soon as he heard her say yes. He took the ring out of the box, put it on her finger and pulled her up against his chest wrapping his arms around her body. Finally, Nick kissed her with a long-awaited kiss. Her body was pressed against his solid chest and the chemistry between them exploded. He turned, picked up the bottle of wine and his glass, then took her hand after she picked up her glass.

Nick and Rocki eagerly walked upstairs to the master bedroom.

He intended to make love to her all night long. Rocki was exactly the woman he'd been looking for all these years. She was unquestionably the right woman for him. A perfect *Life Match*.

"You are both my *Mr. Right* and my *Mr. Wrong*. I love you." Rocki smiled up at him and knew it was going to be the best Christmas she'd ever had!

"Merry Christmas, Rocki." Nick pulled her into his arms in the doorway to the bedroom.

"Merry Christmas, Nick." Rocki kissed him as they made their way to the bed that promised many hours of love and pleasure through the long Christmas night and for many years to come.

# ABOUT THE AUTHOR
## ROSE MARIE MEUWISSEN

Rose Marie Meuwissen, a first-generation Norwegian American born and raised in Minnesota, always tries to incorporate her Norwegian heritage into her writing. After receiving a BA in Marketing from Concordia University, a Masters in Creative Writing from Hamline University soon followed. Minnesota is still where she calls home.

She has traveled around the world, including Scandinavia, but still has many places to see, enjoys attending Scandinavian events, writing conferences and is usually busy writing Christmas Poems, Minnesota Lakes and Nordic Contemporary Romances, Viking Time Travel Romances or Norwegian Traditions Children's Books.

Visit her at www.rosemariemeuwissen.com or www.realnorwegianseatlutefisk.com.

## NOVELS:

- *Taking Chances*—a contemporary romance novel set in Minnesota and Arizona.
- *Married by Saturday*—a contemporary romance novel set in Minnesota and Montana.
- *Accidental Vegas Bride*—a contemporary romance novel set in Minnesota and Nevada.
- *Looking for Mr. Right*—a contemporary internet dating romance novel set on Prior Lake in Minnesota.

# NOVELLAS:

- *Annika—A Christmas Romance*—a contemporary romance set in Minnesota with a Nordic theme during the Christmas Holidays.
- *Skol! Viking Blonde Ale*—a contemporary romance set in Minnesota at an Autumn festival complete with a fortune teller, ale and Vikings!
- *Choosing to Live*—a Norwegian woman's journey during WWII to survive the Nazi Occupation of Norway—*Coming soon!*

# MINNESOTA LAKES ROMANCE NOVELETTES:

- *A Kiss Under the Northern Lights*—a Summer romance set in Ely, Minnesota on Big Lake.
- *Dancing in the Moonlight*—a Summer romance set in Malmo, Minnesota on Mille Lacs Lake.
- *Hot Summer Nights*—a Summer romance set in Prior Lake, Minnesota on Prior Lake.
- *Railroad Ties*—an Autumn romance set in Two Harbors, Minnesota on Lake Superior.
- *Blizzard of Love*—a Winter romance set in Lutsen, Minnesota on Lake Superior.
- *A Norwegian Gift of Love*—a Spring romance set in Minneapolis, Minnesota on Lake Harriet.
- *Old Yule Log Fires*—a Christmas romance set in Excelsior, Minnesota on Lake Minnetonka.
- *A Date for Valentine's Day*—a Valentine romance set in Minnetonka Beach, Minnesota at the Lafayette Country Club on Lake Minnetonka.
- *Dance of Love*—a Fall Festival romance set at the Renaissance Fair in Shakopee, Minnesota.

- ***Lakes, Loons & Lutefisk***—a Hotdish romance set at Looney Days Festival on Loon Lake in Vergas, Minnesota.

# CHILDREN'S BOOKS—REAL NORWEGIAN'S SERIES:

- *Real Norwegians Eat Lutefisk*—a Children's book about the tradition of Lutefisk presented in both English and Norwegian.
- *Real Norwegians Eat Rømmegrøt*—the second Children's book in the series about the tradition of Rømmegrøt presented in both English and Norwegian.
- *Real Norwegians Eat Lefse*—the third Children's book in the series about the tradition of Lefse presented in both English and Norwegian.
- *Real Norwegians Eat Krumkake*—the fourth Children's book in the series about the tradition of Krumkake presented in both English and Norwegian—*Coming next!*

# MINI NOVELETTE—COMING SOON!

- ***Christmas Notes***—a collection of Christmas prose poems to warm the heart during the Christmas season.

# PREVIEW: ACCIDENTAL VEGAS BRIDE

**Continue Reading for a Preview of:**

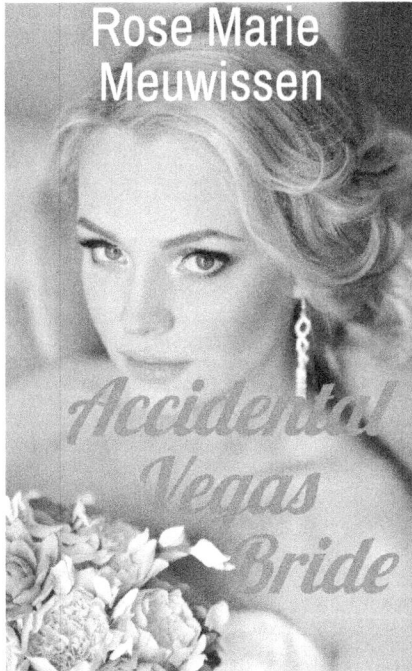

# ACCIDENTAL VEGAS BRIDE

## BY

**Rose Marie Meuwissen**

# COPYRIGHT: ACCIDENTAL VEGAS BRIDE

COPYRIGHT: ACCIDENTAL VEGAS BRIDE

Print ISBN: 978-1-954030-02-2
Published in the United States of America
Nordic Publishing
Edited by Leanore Elliot
Cover Design by Rose Marie Meuwissen

# BLURB: ACCIDENTAL VEGAS BRIDE

After six years of dating and no marriage proposal, Alli broke up with Sam. Getting out of town, on the weekend of Sam's thirtieth birthday, wasn't in her plans. Surprisingly, it sounded like the right choice since it allowed her to be as far away as possible from Sam and Minneapolis on that specific date.

Vegas would do nicely.

It wasn't that Sam didn't love Alli, because he did. But, starting a family was a big commitment that he didn't think he was ready to make, just yet. Six months later, neither had made *the call* and his birthday simply wouldn't be the same without her. When Sam's best friend suggested celebrating his birthday in Vegas, he agreed.

Maybe then he could stop thinking about Alli for a few days.

Anything can happen in Vegas! Surely there was some truth to the saying—*What happens in Vegas, stays in Vegas.*

# ACCIDENTAL VEGAS BRIDE

by

*Rose Marie Meuwissen*

# ACCIDENTAL VEGAS BRIDE
## CHAPTER 1

"This is going to be fun. Right?" Alli asked as she closed her suitcase.

"We *are* going to have the time of our lives," Susie answered, pulling her suitcase toward the door. "And don't forget, what happens in Vegas, stays in Vegas."

"Time of our lives? I could certainly use that but I will settle for fun," Alli stated. She lifted her suitcase off the bed and rolled it over to the door.

"We are going to have fun, you can count on it. Ready?" Susie asked and opened the door. They walked out to the garage and loaded the suitcases in the trunk.

"Are you sure we have everything?" Alli asked while she mentally tried to go over all the things she packed, in case she'd forgotten anything.

"Sure enough. If we forgot something, we can get it in Vegas."

They both got in the car. Susie backed the car out of the garage, drove down the street taking the entrance ramp onto the freeway.

"Right. Okay, fun it is!" Alli said.

"And don't forget, what happens in Vegas, stays in Vegas," Susie repeated.

"Of course, you know that isn't true."

"Well, if it isn't, it should be," Susie stated. "All kinds of crazy things go on in Vegas. People do things they would never even think of doing at home."

"I could never do something I wouldn't be able to talk about the next day."

"Promise me you will let your hair down a little and try to have some fun at least," Susie suggested.

"Heaven knows, I need to relax and have some fun. After I broke up with Sam, I completely lost my desire to date again. It's especially hard when you are still in love with the person you just broke up with. But it is over and I need to move on. I know I need to, but it's so hard." Alli looked out the window at the Mall of America as they drove by at sixty miles an hour. Thank heavens they had a ten o'clock morning flight and hadn't had to get up in the middle of the night simply to catch a flight.

"There will be lots of men in Vegas," Susie offered. "Men looking for a good time. And that is what you need. Someone who will make you laugh again."

"You think I should find some guy and do what with him? Spend the night with him?" Alli asked.

"You're not a virgin or anything like that, so why not?" Susie asked.

"Because it's wrong. It's not good for anyone. Especially me. Having sex with a strange man is not going to happen. Trust me, it won't."

"Okay, you do whatever makes you happy and I'll do the same." Susie parked the car in the long-term parking area at the airport.

They walked into the airport with bags in tow and proceeded to the security area to get in line. Once through the screening process which always was a pain, food was next on their list. They stopped at the French Meadows Café, purchased salads for later on the plane to go along with chocolate croissants for breakfast and then made their way to Caribou Coffee to get some much-needed caffeine.

"Some days, having this cup of mocha cappuccino makes the

whole day worth getting up for," Susie said sipping her multi flavored highly caffeinated beverage of choice for the morning.

"I will give you that one." Alli sipped her mint chocolate flavored cappuccino as they sat and waited at the gate for their flight.

"It's too bad Jennifer and Kally had to take a later flight," Susie stated.

"They will only be a few hours behind us. We'll meet them at the Monte Carlo Hotel. We can go ahead and check in, change into our swimsuits and head to the pool. I told them we would be there as soon as we checked into our room. You okay with that?"

"Don't you want to gamble first? Maybe win a jackpot or two before they get there," Susie asked.

"First of all, the odds of winning any money in Vegas are slim to none. I'm not giving them my money for nothing in return. Hell, I'd rather get something for my money. That's why I'll opt for shopping over gambling."

"You are no fun at all!"

"Really? You do the math, have you ever came out ahead with how much you spent, versus how much you won?" Alli asked.

"Probably not. But it always feels good when you win a large jack-pot. Well, maybe not large to some people but $1,000 is large to me. I usually come out ahead but not by much. Last time it was only by $100. It is by far better than coming out behind."

"That's one way to look at it."

"Fine. We can go to the pool first," Susie said.

"Don't sound so disappointed. The casinos are open all night but the sun goes down early this time of year."

Finally, they were in line to board and followed the other passengers to their seats. As they walked down the narrow aisle between the seats on the airplane, they pulled their suitcases behind them with their large purses resting on one of their shoulders.

The line boarding the plane moved slowly, so Alli took the time to scan the plane to see if she thought there were any good-looking men on the plane, she might be interested in even chatting with in person.

Unfortunately, she didn't find a single one. She hoped Vegas would offer a better, more interesting selection choice.

Once they were in the air, they ate their goodies from the French Meadow Café. Reading on planes was one of Alli's favorite things to do. Although, she was a bit old fashioned and brought her paperback romance novel along to read. Someone deserved the wedding and the happily ever after even though it wouldn't be her.

Las Vegas airport was crowded and Susie insisted on stopping at a group of slot machines that greeted them as soon as they walked off the plane.

Alli waited patiently while Susie dropped a quick $20 in one and came up empty handed. Why Susie never learned, Alli had no idea.

Alli found herself checking out the men for the first time in six months. It had been six months and she needed to do this. One guy caught her appraising him and smiled at her. She wasn't sure she could do this. She kept on walking and didn't look back at him. It wasn't surprising she found herself looking for someone who looked like Sam. She knew she couldn't replace him, what she needed was to look for someone who looked totally different so she wouldn't be reminded of Sam every time she looked at him. Sam was perfect for her in every way except for the minor little detail that he didn't want to get married yet, or have a family.

Time was running out for her and he unquestionably didn't understand how her biological clock was ticking away and she didn't have that much time left. She had just turned thirty before they broke up and she had tried to make him understand she simply couldn't wait any longer. All he said was that he was sorry but he wasn't ready to start a family. Now to top it all off, today was Sam's 30th birthday. She had planned to have a big birthday party for him, in fact she'd already began planning it, never thinking she wouldn't be there for it.

Which was why she had finally agreed to go on this Vegas trip. She didn't think she could stay in Minneapolis tonight, knowing it was his birthday today and someone had probably planned a big 30th birthday bash for him. And she was not invited. Had she really thought she would be invited, as the ex-girlfriend? No, of course not. But she had really wanted to be there. She really wanted to be with Sam, but he hadn't called her since their break up. He had broken off all contact with her and since he hadn't called her, she refused to call him, which led to a Mexican standoff. Neither one of them had made the call.

Susie signed the paperwork for their car rental and they took the elevator down to pick up the car. Alli hadn't been paying attention to how the conversation had gone between Susie and the car rental agent, so needless to say she was quite shocked to find out their rental was a Mustang convertible.

"Really? What were you thinking Susie? A convertible?" Alli asked staring at the car.

"I guess they were really wiped out of cars, so this is what they gave us. It's our lucky day. I think we need to go hit the slots," Susie said.

"Of course, you do," Alli said as they loaded the suitcases in the trunk of the Mustang and got in the car. She was silent while they drove to the hotel.

"You, okay?" Susie asked. "You are awfully quiet."

"It's Sam's 30th birthday today," Alli stated.

"I totally forgot. You never said anything. That's why you agreed to come to Vegas isn't it?"

"Yes. I was afraid I would call him or do something much worse like going over to his townhouse," Alli stated.

"No chance of that happening now. Promise me you won't call him this weekend."

"I promise. It's over. He obviously hasn't changed his mind since he never called me."

They parked and checked in the hotel. Alli couldn't believe her ears when she heard the clerk offer Susie a suite since it was the only room, they had available with double beds due to a large convention being held at the hotel. She then heard the desk clerk say if they were looking for single men, the convention attendees were 95% men. What were the odds? Maybe she would meet someone really nice this weekend if their lucky streak held up.

An hour later, they were at the pool in their already pre-tanned bikini clad trim bodies, stretched out on the chaise lounges with a couple of frozen strawberry margaritas surrounded by chair after chair filled with hot men.

Made in the USA
Coppell, TX
12 February 2025

45804648R00132